For ROUENNA

For ROUENNA

Sigrid Nunez

FARRAR, STRAUS AND GIROUX

NEW YORK

FARRAR, STRAUS AND GIROUX
19 Union Square West, New York 10003

Printed in the United States of America
FIRST EDITION, 2001

Library of Congress Cataloging-in-Publication Data
Nunez, Sigrid.
    For Rouenna / Sigrid Nunez.—1st ed.
        p. cm.
    ISBN 0-374-25430-3 (hardcover : alk. paper)
    1. Female friendship—Fiction.   2. Vietnamese Conflict,
1961–1975—Medical care—Fiction.   3. Women authors—Fiction.
4. Nurses—Fiction.   5. Death—Fiction.   I. Title.

PS3564.U475 F6 2001
813'.54—dc21

                                    2001033696

Designed by Gretchen Achilles

Part ONE

After my first book was published, I received some letters. Most of them were from strangers, people who had read the book and who wanted me to know what they thought of it. They were friendly letters for the most part, though a few were critical. ("I hope you won't mind my saying that I did not like the ending at all," and so on.) I also heard from people I had known in the past. Near strangers: people I had not been in touch with for twenty, thirty years and whom I rarely if ever still thought about. Almost every one of these letters began with an expression of doubt that I would remember the sender, and my letters in reply always began with an assurance that I did remember, which was the truth. Even before I opened one of these letters, I would recognize the name written above the return address on the envelope. (Sometimes I recognized the handwriting.) Almost always unfamiliar, though, was the return address itself. These old acquaintances of mine, these ghosts from my past, had moved away from the places where I had known them, some very far. One of the few letters from the state of New York had been mailed from a men's penitentiary. Sometimes the writer wrote PERSONAL on the envelope, or PERSONAL AND CONFIDENTIAL. "I hope you will remember my sorry ass," the letter from the inmate began, "now that it has landed in jail."

Unlike the ones I received from strangers, these letters were not usually about my book. In fact, often the writer had not read the book but had only heard of it, from a review, say, and had been moved to get in touch "after all these years." These letters tended to be long—three or four pages—and filled with autobiographical detail. They took me back—to college, to high school, and even further. I heard from three women who had been my best friends in seventh grade. (Most of the people I heard from were women.) Rarely was I surprised to learn what had become of people. They had married. They had had children. The jobs they were in were the jobs I might have predicted for them. It was their wanting to tell me all this that surprised me and that I found poignant.

I answered every letter. And usually that was the end of it. I would not hear from the person again, or if I did it was just once more. A much shorter letter might come; a postcard. One of the friends from seventh grade dug up and sent an old photograph, me at thirteen, along with a copy of a poem in my own juvenile hand, which I threw away, unread, remembering only too well the kind of poem I wrote at thirteen.

Time passed. A year, another year, enough time for me to finish another book—a long period when no such letters came. And then one day there came one more. ("I don't know if you remember me.") From Brooklyn this time. And this time I did not remember.

I did not remember a Rouenna Zycinski. I was sure I had never known her. But many years ago, according to her letter, we had been neighbors in the same public housing project, on Staten Island. She was older than I, this woman, the same age as my elder sister, and she remembered her, and my other sister, and my mother and father. She gave everyone's name and the number of the building we had lived in and the apartment number—she gave all this information in her letter, and it was all accurate. That world—the world of the projects—I had written about in my first book, which she had just read. The book had brought that world back to her, had brought back many memories, and that was all she wanted to say.

I answered the letter right away, thanking her for writing, and then I forgot about her, until a few weeks later, she wrote again. We were, she said (hardly accurately this time, in my opinion), neighbors once more. Brooklyn, Manhattan. Two stops on the L train. A matter of minutes. Could we meet?

I did not want to. I had no desire to meet this woman. She was a stranger, and I am wary of strangers. Ours was only the slenderest connection. Not even her name rang a bell. She and her family had moved out of the projects *some forty years ago*. My own family had moved out ten years later. Why should we meet? I could think of no good reason. And I had the uneasy feeling that this woman wanted something—something more than just to meet. I could not say what it was, but I sensed that there might be some danger—no, *danger* is melodramatic—some trouble that could come of meeting her, and I had enough trouble. Had she been a man, I do not think it would have been hard for me to say no. But a peculiar sense of obligation nagged me, as if I owed this woman, this perfect stranger from the margins of my book of memories—but what could I possibly owe her?

I had enough trouble. The arrival of this woman's letters coincided with an odd time in my life—an unhappy time. When her first letter came, I had just broken up with a man I had been living with for several years. I had moved out of the apartment we'd shared (*his* apartment before we met) and into a new one. I was alone. (She was alone, too; though she did not say so, I could not imagine Rouenna Zycinski except living all alone, those two subway stops away in Brooklyn.) Midway through unpacking, I had lost heart and quit. I was living in disarray, half out of boxes—I hardly knew where anything was. The kitchen was bare, I had not yet once used the stove—I went out for everything, from morning coffee to midnight drink. I went out alone—I was avoiding people. I was avoiding having to explain that G. and I were no longer together. I was avoiding having to answer questions about my work, about how my next book was going, and having to explain that it was not going, I had abandoned that book. I had not written anything for months. I'd had to move quickly and was forced to take more or less the first place I saw. Two small rooms that even put together would not have made one large one. The sofa here, the bed there, and no more space. The floor was splintery, the light was—well, there was no light. Almost all the tenants in the building were women. The landlord would not rent to single men or to families (not that it was easy to imagine any family squeezing into one of the cramped apartments that had been carved out of that once-elegant townhouse). So we were mostly women; I had young women living on all sides. I had forgotten how much young women cry. And it seemed I was not the only one with romantic troubles. I often heard couples fighting—how my pulse would surge whenever I heard that. And once, an anguished male voice bellowed up and down the air shaft—*I love you, you bitch!*—and I burst into tears.

In that building also were many cats. I think every woman had one. (Dogs were not allowed—the landlord had the same low opinion of dogs as he had of single men.) Coming home sometimes I would glance up at the facade of the building and see the familiar curvaceous silhouette in almost every other window. My own cat prowled the cluttered rooms with wide, disbelieving eyes. At first he meowed a lot, as if imploring me . . . Then he grew silent and grave, as (I supposed) the truth sank in: the order that he was accustomed to and needed and loved did not follow wherever we went but belonged to that other life, the one we had left behind forever.

Instead of making order, instead of settling down in my new place and getting on with life, I dreamed of going away. I had read Marguerite Yourcenar's account of how she had traveled by train across the United States, writing portions of her masterpiece, *Memoirs of Hadrian.* "Closed inside my compartment as if in a cubicle of some Egyptian tomb, I worked late into the night between New York and Chicago; then all the next day, in the restaurant of a Chicago station . . . then again until dawn, alone in the observation car of a Sante Fé limited." Page after page of this work that had given her so much difficulty for so many years now poured out of her, and: "I can hardly recall a day spent with more ardor, or more lucid nights."

Irresistible fantasy. New York to California. I would visit S. in San Francisco. *Days of ardor. Lucid nights.* Writing as I had never done before.

Irresistible fantasy: the look on G.'s face when I told him. It had been one of his chief complaints: I was incapable of just the sort of act I was now contemplating. I had no sense of adventure, I was the least spontaneous person alive. ("Someone says to you let's have sex, and you say just a minute I have to go make out my will.") If I did not do more—go out, travel, see more of the world, get more experience of life—I would end up having nothing to write about. It had been one of the last things he had said to me before we broke up (though he was hardly saying it to me for the first time), and the way he said it, that final time, I felt as if he were putting a curse on me.

It was not the sort of trip that people made anymore—certainly not alone. I was told that my fellow passengers would be mostly families. And things were different now than they had been in the forties. Now there would be music, or Muzak, playing in that Chicago station restaurant. Nor would Yourcenar likely find herself alone in that observation car. The trains were almost always crowded now, rarely quiet, hardly the place for reading, let alone writing masterpieces. Always the sound of someone's chatter or snoring, the tinny music coming out of other people's Walkmans, or the beeps and quacks of someone's computer game—this, at least, had been my own experience riding trains in recent years. The filth of the toilets. The bad food. The families with young children in neighboring compartments. "Will all the compartments be full?" I asked the booking agent. "Oh, yes. And you'd better make up your mind fast. We book these trains ten months in advance."

So much for spontaneity.

But I had fallen into one of those writer's traps: I had let myself become convinced that in order to begin writing again I needed to be elsewhere—preferably somewhere I had never been before. I wanted to write about us, about G. and me, how we came together, how we came apart. But it was too soon, probably. And anyway I had promised never to . . .

Still, I wanted to go away. It didn't have to be such a big deal, I told myself. I would go anywhere I did not have to hear young women cry. I thought of renting a house for a month or so somewhere in the country. But it was winter. I saw myself cold, snowbound. And how would I get around? Not only did I not have a car, I did not know how to drive.

The train trip, the house in the country. A journey, a retreat. A place to grieve. A place to write. Irresistible fantasies, but in the end I never went anywhere. I stayed home and finished unpacking. G. was right about me then. But he had reminded me of something. As soon as I was finally settled in my new home, for the first time in my life I made out a will.

I did not answer the woman's second letter right away. I put it off for weeks. She had given me her telephone number, but instead of calling I wrote again. I said that she had caught me at a busy time, but perhaps in a month or so . . .

In a month to the day, she wrote again. I saw that it would be useless not to call. It was no longer a question of putting this duty off but of getting it over with.

I had expected she would come to me, in Manhattan. I had several places in mind to suggest for us to meet. Instead, to my dismay, she invited me to lunch at her Brooklyn apartment. A breathy, slightly stammering voice: she sounded both flustered and excited. She sounded as if she was afraid I would say no. I said that I would bring dessert. And that Saturday—a cold gray day with a little dry snow blowing—reluctantly, still fearing some obscure trouble, still burdened with that peculiar sense of obligation and now also with a chocolate mousse pie, I took the L train to Williamsburg.

I was early—I am usually early for appointments (a habit that always irked G., who saw it not as the virtue of punctuality but as a neurotic fear of being late). We really did live only minutes apart, this woman and I, and in my usual (punctual or neurotic) way I had allowed almost an hour for the trip. In those few minutes, though, the weather had changed. I climbed the subway stairs into sun. The snow had stopped. It was a different kind of day entirely—a good day for a walk. And it was while I was walking, careful not to swing the cake box too vigorously, that my mood started to lift.

I knew this neighborhood. I knew several people who lived here, all artists. It had been one of my first thoughts about this woman, that she too might be one of the hundreds of artists who had settled in this part of Brooklyn over the past fifteen years. Easy to recognize, from the style of their clothes and hair and even their backpacks, they thronged the streets that bright Saturday noon, easy to tell from the Italian, Polish, and Latino immigrants they threatened soon to displace. (Displacement anxiety: in the subway station, a sign taped to a post: a woman looking for someone to share her loft: SMOKERS OK, BUT ABSOLUTELY NO WALL STREET YUPPIE TYPES!)

On my walk I went north, into Greenpoint. I remembered the first time I had ever been to Greenpoint, almost ten years before, and had gone into a grocery to buy tea. When I asked the man behind the counter where to find the tea, he pressed his palms together like a priest and shook his head: no English. That store was there still; I paused to look in the window, filled with Polish specialties, and wondered whether the man ever had learned English. To do so, he would have had only to cross the street, where then as now an English language school stood. On the other hand, so long as he never left that neighborhood, there was no real need. Polish was spoken everywhere—in the stores, in the bank, in the health and beauty clinics. Walking through the park, I heard two men arguing in Polish, children playing jacks in Polish, and an ardent young couple sitting on a park bench, making Polish love.

And, on the side of a bus stop shelter, someone had felt-penned this:

Q. *What did the Polish artist do?*
A. *He moved to SoHo.*

But none of this had anything to do with my mood, any more than did the change of weather. It was something that had occurred to me—now that I was actually about to meet this woman. Until this moment I had not really given her much thought. Only now did I begin to wonder seriously about her. She was not an artist, I decided. She would not be like one of them or like any of my other friends—she was from another world entirely. The voyeur in me was aroused. Would she really turn out to live alone as I'd imagined, or would there be a roommate, a lover, family? What would her apartment be like, and what did she do for a living? I saw that it would not be hard for me to get through this visit—all I'd have to do would be to eat and listen. For it was not about me that the woman would want to talk, but about herself—I was quite sure of this. I had come to expect it from the kind of people who got in touch with me. That letter from the penitentiary was a full confession—thirty pages in which that old high school boyfriend of mine poured out the whole sad sordid tale of how he'd got there. Rouenna Zycinski, too, wanted to tell me how she'd got where she was. She hadn't done so in her letters—she had said nothing about herself. She was saving her story for when we met. So my thought went. And as I turned around and headed back toward the street where she lived, I found myself intensely curious, and curiosity always perks me up.

Her building was near the subway. A three-story frame house with green vinyl siding, graceless, homely almost to the point of grimness, like most of the buildings around it; like most of Brooklyn. As I rang the bell, the yellowish-gray curtains of a window on the ground floor stirred, and a yellowish-gray head appeared: a woman, the landlady perhaps, keeping an eye out, or just some nosy neighbor. But when I nodded at her, she made a frightful face and withdrew, angrily jerking the curtain shut.

Inside, it smelled of roasted meat.

"Hello? Up here—I'm up here." That nervous, breathy voice. I climbed the stairs toward it. She stood in the doorway—she filled the doorway, she was so stout. Her face was flushed, from cooking perhaps, or from nervousness, or stoutness—I didn't know—but she was all red, unnaturally red. No, I did not recognize her in the slightest. "I'm Rouenna," she said. Barefoot on a doormat printed with sunflowers. A long, loose, tent-like dress—it too was printed with flowers. The roast-meat smell was coming from here. I handed her the cake box, and she took it shyly, she made a little show of grateful surprise as if she weren't expecting it, though I had said that I would bring dessert when we made our date on the phone. She backed into the apartment, into the overpowering roast-meat smell. "You look just like your photo," she said, and it took me a moment to figure out that she was talking about the photograph on my book jacket. She held the door open for me, she wafted her hand in a gesture of welcome, and I entered her world.

The word *parlor* came to me, so old-fashioned did that living room seem, with its stuffed furniture and bric-a-brac, its doilies and afghans and needlepoint. A tall birdcage in a nook by the window held a pair of dozing parakeets. Fake Persian rugs, curtains of moss-green velour—it was the kind of place that makes me want to sneeze, no matter how tidy it is. The kind of place that makes me go a little weak in the knees—I who have lived in rooms so meagerly furnished people visiting for the first time assumed I had just moved in. The Japanese are my heroes in this regard and, closer to home, the Shakers. *Neurotic*, again, was how G. saw this *fear of decoration*. But think of it as a way to avoid what always happens: how one possession always leads to another, and how this goes on and on, complicating life until, in no time at all, what we own ends up owning us.

It was summer in that parlor: hot and humid. The windows were opaque with steam. I went weak in the knees right there. The throbbing busyness of the place—all that *stuff*—the heat, the heavy smell—Rouenna herself—all that floral-printed flesh. I sank onto a chair whose cushion gave under me like a feather bed. My misgivings returned. What was I doing there? On a coffee table, among full candy dishes, magazines fanned out as in a dentist's office, a stack of plastic coasters, and a giant kidney-shaped ashtray was my book.

Something to drink, offered Rouenna. I asked for anything fizzy and cold, and she fixed me a ginger ale with ice.

She had cooked, of all things, a turkey. She seemed embarrassed about this. But it was her habit to cook large meals on weekends, she said. She would give part of the turkey to the woman downstairs—not the landlady, as it turned out, but a frail, addled old widow who could barely take care of herself. And some of the turkey would go to the church, where every week volunteers fed Sunday dinner to the homeless.

A good heart. And here I had been inwardly sneering—no, *sneering* is too harsh—I had been shaking my head at her. I sipped my iced drink to cool my shame. Rouenna went back into the kitchen and returned with a tray of different cheeses, crackers, and olives—enough for a meal in itself. Now, and later, when we sat down to the turkey, I noticed how, like many obese people, Rouenna ate daintily—at least in front of a witness. Of the hors d'oeuvres she ate nothing at all; they were for company—like the giant ashtray, I supposed, since Rouenna did not smoke. I noticed too that, for all her weight, she was quite buoyant, bustling about the table, which stood in a little alcove outside the kitchen, light on her small bare feet. She had been slender once, and her body, under its excess pounds, had not forgotten. (I had seen this before, in the plump but graceful *mesdames* whose photographs from lither days hung in the studios where they now taught ballet.)

It was like Thanksgiving. She had *stuffed* the turkey. She had made gravy and mashed potatoes and peas and cornbread. She must have been cooking since she got up that morning, and she must have got up early. I caught myself shaking my head again. So much food—"lunch" was going to take hours. Rouenna, as I say, ate only small portions of everything, but I ate a lot, as I usually did when the food was good; though nowhere near Rouenna's size, I had already for some time given up trying to be thin.

It turned out she did live alone in that apartment, the rest of which I would see before going home: a bedroom as bright and busy as the living room, with a ruffled paisley bedspread and matching paisley window curtains, and a thick shaggy gold rug like the fleece of the mythic sheep. (A house without books, I noted. Only that one book, mine, on the coffee table.) She had been living in that same apartment for about six years, she said. Before that she had lived in Manhattan. "I had a nice rent-stabilized place in Kips Bay, but after twelve years I was ready for a change. Or maybe I just needed to get back to my roots." She was Brooklyn-born, with grandparents on both sides from Poland. Though she was only joking about getting back to her roots, she had never regretted leaving "snotty Manhattan." This immigrant working-class neighborhood suited her, and she loved the narrow streets and the low skyline, the Italian cafés with their excellent coffee, the small cheap restaurants serving pierogies and boiled beef and borscht. A bakery on every corner, and in every bakery the delicious poppyseed cake that brought back Grandma . . . Rouenna had been happy those six years in Williamsburg, and she said she wished the artists had chosen somewhere else to settle. *To ruin* was what she actually said— as if many of them hadn't beaten her to Williamsburg by many years. All these *artistes*, she said. Moved here supposedly because they were poor, but buying up buildings left and right!

As if these could not possibly be people I would ever know or want to know.

Snotty Manhattan was where she worked still. She was the manager of a women's discount clothing store. She had a car but she took the subway every day, to Thirty-fourth Street. Not an exciting job, she admitted; not a job she loved, but better than other jobs she'd had over the years—and she'd had plenty. Waitressing, bartending, grooming pets. All jobs to get by, to pay the rent. And yet Rouenna had a profession: she was a trained nurse.

I had been right about not being bored that day, and wrong about Rouenna's eagerness to talk about herself; I had to draw her out. At first, she kept trying to draw *me* out. But I was evasive—I had no desire to talk about myself with this strange woman—and in the awkward pauses that fell between us, I watched her struggling, her flushed face turning a deeper, mortified red, as if she was afraid she had offended me. To make it up to her, I kept praising the food, and each time I did so she squirmed and batted her eyes self-consciously. She had unusually pale but intense blue eyes—the one beautiful and still young-looking feature in an otherwise ordinary fiftyish face.

I could not quite see her as a nurse—not with all that weight. But then that time when she had been a nurse was so long past, she herself placed it "in another life."

"If I met that person walking down the street today, I wouldn't recognize her."

"You didn't like being a nurse?"

"Well, back then a girl didn't have many choices."

Three, as I recalled. The others were secretary and school-teacher. My elder sister, the one who was Rouenna's age, had also gone into nursing, also halfheartedly.

"Don't get me wrong," Rouenna said. "I was a good nurse—I did my job. I just didn't last very long. And besides, look at these." She held out her hands. They were small and plump, like her feet. "A nurse really should have large hands."

I had never thought of this. I said, "When did you quit?"

"After I got out of the army."

"You were in the army?"

She nodded once, sharply, with pursed lips.

"What made you join the army?"

"If you enlisted, they helped pay for nursing school," she said, in a tone that suggested that this had been anything but the great deal it might sound like to me. And then she did a very odd thing: she clutched her head between her hands, opened her mouth, and mimed a loud scream.

She had my full attention. I had never known any woman who'd served in the military, and I wanted to hear more. But it was not to be. Rouenna was on her feet, clearing the table. When I got up to help, she patted the air with one of her small plump hands until I sat down again.

I was left alone for a few minutes while she busied herself in the kitchen.

The steam had long since cleared from the windows, and the gray, gauzy light of a late winter day shone into the room. The parakeets were moving about their cage, "a boy and a girl," Rouenna had told me earlier. A blue breast and a yellow breast. She was very fond of them, clearly—proud, even, in that funny way people sometimes are proud of their pets. "They're incredibly smart," she assured me; those chirrups and tweets now filling the air were "them saying that they love each other." I thought of the Polish couple on the park bench. When she first got the birds (a farewell present from the pet store where she used to work), Rouenna had called them Hansel and Gretel. But seeing how they doted on each other, she renamed them Romeo and Juliet. I blushed when she told me this—who knows exactly why. Their love-twitter was pretty—but how would it be, living there alone and hearing it all the time? I glanced toward their nook and saw that they were doing the Balcony Scene—except that it was blue Juliet on the floor of the cage below, gazing up at her yellow Romeo.

What Rouenna really wanted, she said, was a dog. But she couldn't bear the thought of it being cooped up all day while she was at work. Like many bird-lovers, she was not keen on cats.

While we were eating dessert, we talked about the housing project. Neither of us had ever been back. Neither of us could name a single person we had known back then who might still be living there. (By chance, just as Rouenna and I happened to live near each other in New York, our mothers had ended up in neighboring towns in New Jersey; our fathers were both dead.) Milk bottles outside each apartment door, the diaper laundry-man, the traveling knife grinder, the traveling amusement rides, the bread boy going from building to building with his basket of warm loaves. Another life.

We had been to the same grammar school, Rouenna and I, and we remembered many of the same teachers, the diabolical ones in particular. Mr. Zappulla, Miss Holsey, Mr. Fludd—all names to raise the nape-hairs still.

Mr. Zappulla went at boys usually with wood: ruler or yard-stick, pointer or paddle.

Kneeling on marbles with arms raised overhead: to think that pretty young Miss Holsey had devised this.

Mr. Fludd kept a pair of handcuffs in his desk.

We began to laugh. We had to laugh, remembering. Handcuffs! Where were the social workers? Where were our parents? And though I laughed, I felt a familiar darkness come over me. These were true stories; those teachers had really existed, blighting our childhoods and memories of childhood, and I didn't like to think about them. I didn't like that nagging question about our parents.

Some of you aren't even human beings. (Mr. Fludd.) We were animals. And the government had built a zoo (the project) to keep us in. How he hated rock and roll (*jungle music!*) and what he called *colored dancing. Colored laughter* drove him up a wall. *If you can't laugh like a human being you better not dare laugh at all!* (But colored *singing* soothed his soul; no one could sing the way the colored people sang, Mr. Fludd always said.)

Not every teacher was a brute, of course. (No, kind Miss Clyde, I have not forgotten.) But I had discovered that the more time passed, the grimmer those early school days appeared to me. I seemed to remember only the bad. And this was the darkness that would come over me: an unhappiness that was at least partly self-pity. A fear, the awful fear that, back then and there, children's lives had been spoiled before they'd fairly begun.

"And do you remember Mrs. Coniglio?" she asked.

Of course I did: a broad, creased face and large red rough hands and a long-suffering, diffident mien: the janitress. She wore her gray hair in a black hairnet. There was a shame attached to her: the shame of illiteracy. She appeared with her mop and pail whenever a child threw up or wet the floor. She saved the shavings she collected each day from the pencil sharpeners and sprinkled them over the mess before mopping up. The children liked her, she was gentle and mute, the rare adult who never raised hand or voice. To Mr. Fludd she was an object lesson. As soon as she and her mop were gone, we would be warned. That's what would become of *us* if we didn't learn to read and write. We'd spend our lives like Mrs. Coniglio, cleaning up pee-pee and puke.

Dusk settled, and we talked on, and the whole time we were talking it was as if some third presence also were there, right in the room with us, some quivering invisible thing that passed over and around and between us. Invisible winged thing like a great moth or butterfly . . . always just on the point of landing when it took off again. A whirring thing—I could almost hear it. Restless. Uncanny. Frustrating.

But it was time to go. Rouenna would not let me help with the dishes. And I had to be very firm about not wanting to take any food home with me. "But what are you going to do for dinner?" she asked, and I, having eaten enough for two days, just laughed.

Before I left, though, I had to sign my book for her. She was shy about asking for this; she waited until I had already put on my coat. I sat back down on the soft chair and opened the book. I was inscribing it to her, I was writing her name—*R* I wrote and then *o*—when the thing that had been there all afternoon, the whirring, circling, maddening thing, at last came to light. There followed a moment of acute, vertiginous strangeness. I squeezed the pen, staring down as from a height at those letters, the *R* and the *o.* Then I collected myself, pressed down firmly with the pen, and finished writing. I closed the book, replaced it on the coffee table, and left as quickly as I could.

Outside, it was dark and cold—freezing, after the steamy apartment—and I hurried through the streets as if someone were chasing me.

Roro. A tall sinewy girl with a thatch of dirty-blond hair. One of those my mother always referred to as "little hoydens," wild things, girls who caused and attracted trouble. The train was coming—I could hear it as I approached the subway station—and I raced to catch it. I slipped through the closing doors and sat down heavily, queasy from all that running, all that agitation on such a full stomach.

Roro. Why hadn't she told me that's who she was? How could I possibly be expected to recognize her in the woman who called herself Rouenna? And what must she be thinking now—after the way I had bolted? Our good-byes were a blur—had I even thanked her? Had she guessed that I'd finally remembered her?

But it wasn't true. Though I now knew who she was, I only just barely remembered Rouenna Zycinski. My parents and my sisters would have remembered her, but I was too young. No: what I remembered was a story about her. It was a terrible story, one that would have been hard to forget even if it hadn't been told over and over, long after Roro and her family had moved away. Something had happened one hot summer day—something I persisted for years in believing I had witnessed. In fact, I was not there that day—it was a trick of memory, I was told. I had only heard the story, later, from the many who *were* there.

But how about other people's memories playing tricks on them? How else explain the fact that I remember everything, and so minutely? It is summer, it is a blazing afternoon, and the Big

Playground is as crowded as it ever gets. Children in swimsuits run squealing under the showers, basketball is in progress, and every place on every bench is taken, often by a woman with a baby carriage. It is noisy, what with the children playing, and cars driving by with radios blaring, and the loud motor and incessant carillon of the ice cream truck parked nearby. It is so hot the ice cream runs down your knuckles almost as soon as the man puts the cone in your hand. A scream cuts through the noise—a high scream like a bright red Frisbee rides the hot dense air—and the playground goes still. Now in the stillness two distinct sounds can be heard. One high, one deep; screaming, shouting; a girl, a man. The door of one of the apartment buildings opens, and the girl tears out. Screaming, naked. Behind her, almost upon her, comes her half-naked father. Barefoot, shirtless, pants slipping down his hips because he wears no belt, because the belt is in his hand, he is swinging the belt over his head, he is cracking the belt on the air. *"Cunt! You goddamn cunt, I'll kill you, you little cunt!"* She believes him. No one hearing her screams could doubt it. She flies before him as before sure death. But where can she go— a terrified naked child—and no one moves, no one tries to stop them, to get between them; all stand as if bewitched, frozen, as in the game we call Statues. Always she keeps a safe stride ahead but is almost caught as she rounds the seesaws. *Crack!* She must have felt at least the tip that time. What a sprinter she is, how she veers on a dime, all bright pink fleetness, like a skinned rabbit. Round the seesaws and back the way she came, fists clenched, elbows and knees pumping impossibly fast *and she is still scream- ing she never stops screaming never stops running streaking past all those astonished eyes dashing back through the door—*

Cunt!

Pandemonium in the playground. Small children mill and shriek. The boys on the basketball court begin hooting like apes. *Did you see, man? Oh man, did you see?* It has made their day, it has made their summer. I see their grinning apish faces, I see other faces blank with shock—and that *isn't* me standing by the ice cream truck, chocolate streaming down my knuckles, watching, hearing the ice cream man mutter *Jesus Mary and Joseph* under his breath?

And so the word—the ugliest word in the English language—enters my vocabulary. Or at least in memory word and story are linked.

The story was kept alive, told and retold, became part of the bleak history of that time and place, that dark corner of America where the beacon of Dr. Spock failed to penetrate.

Later, the story got mixed up with other stories that had violence and nakedness in them, some true, some not. Movies about reform schools and prisons. Shaved heads, uniforms, hose baths. Whips and flesh. Pornography. Documentary. Somewhere the grainy black-and-white image of naked women driven by storm troopers through a wood. That was another bright sunny day: dappled light, leafy shade.

The train sat still: the power had died, and we were stuck between stations. We sat waiting, helpless in the dark. It was so dark, I could not make out the man sitting across from me; so still, I could hear him sigh. And out of this dark stillness came words I had read—something about a scream hanging over a village, the poet's childhood home. *Its pitch would be the pitch of my village.* And I thought of my scream—I mean Roro's scream, hanging in the blue sky over the project, there still and forever, hanging over my—over our—childhood, and as the lights flickered and the train hummed to life, I remembered the odd thing Rouenna had done, at the table, clutching her head between her hands and opening her mouth so wide—

Light flooded the car, dazzling after the blackout, revealing that the man sitting across from me was not a man at all but a woman trying to look like a man, and a he-man at that: buzz cut, toothpick, work boots.

At my stop, when I got off the train, I had a moment's shock as I glimpsed G. hurrying along the platform across the tracks. But it was not G.—G. was not even in town that day. (Not the first time this had happened to me. Said often to happen after someone has died—the dead one sighted countless times by the living. Making sense, I supposed: in a way you could say that G. was now dead to me.)

It was not long after the incident in the playground that Roro and her family moved out of the project.

She no longer called herself Roro. But then I was not known by my childhood name anymore, either.

A quiet evening. No messages, and the phone never rang. I got into bed early and read. Unable to concentrate, I turned out the light. I began to cry. Every night since losing G., no matter what kind of day it had been, no matter what kind of mood I was in, when I turned out the light I would cry—not the noisy, stormy sobbing of my young neighbors, still capable of being outraged at their own suffering, but the silent tears of one old enough to be their mother.

I lay a long time without sleeping. I was where I did not want to be: I was back in school. I was in the lunchroom. Old Miss Hazel on duty. Assistant principal. Good Catholic, every day to mass. The powder lay thick on her face, which was why, according to my mother, the ashes stayed on her forehead long after the priest had put them there—almost halfway through Lent. Tapping a fingernail on the table next to my lunch tray. "You didn't eat your pear." No. After the canned beans and franks, after the canned sliced beets, I had no stomach for canned pear. And now I was quaking. Witch Hazel: scariest of a scary bunch. *You think you're so tough, you little snot-noses. Just try something, you wise guys, you guttersnipes, you punks. You'll see what you get from me. And remember, I've been through two wars.* Always this reminder, how the horrors of two world wars had prepared her for us. Once, a stray cat appeared in the schoolyard, where Witch Hazel would not have it. *Give it a good swift kick, see if that won't get rid of it.* Thick as thieves with Mr. Fludd, she shared his deepest need: to turn colored laughter into colored tears.

I told the truth. "If I eat that pear, I'll throw up."

"Is that so?" *Tap tap tap* the whole time, as if she were simultaneously translating into Morse code. Lowering her face so near mine, I could smell the powder. Big smile. *"Well, eat it and throw up."*

"This little girl must have a virus," she told Mrs. Coniglio.

My mother was called to fetch me home, and the kids at my table had to stay after school. *Teach them to scream and jump out of their seats like that.*

Old Witch Hazel. Good Catholic. Cunt. If the hell that her kind invented exists, that is where she must be. Canned colored laughter at earsplitting volume is piped into her cell at all times. Good swift kicks are her daily lot, cats shit where she sleeps, and her food is canned ashes and canned spewed pear.

Later that night, I was back in Brooklyn. I saw Rouenna, sleepless in her own bed, tossing and turning, struggling with a demon. One o'clock, two o'clock. Finally, bested, she throws off the covers and gets up. She pads to the kitchen, so soft on her plump feet not a floorboard creaks. Past the star-cross'd pair snuggling breast to breast in their cage over which Rouenna has fitted, for the night, an old stained nylon half slip. In the kitchen, without turning on the light, she opens the refrigerator, and by the glow of the tiny bulb her face is pale, her mouth set as she beholds the bulging shelves. At the crackle of tinfoil, the parakeets stir. She does not bother to remove the dishes, she does not pull up a chair. She stands, leaning into the refrigerator, and eats. There in the cool spotlight she feasts—to hell with the widow downstairs, the homeless, the hungry. *She* is hungry! No one has ever been so hungry as she, so desperate for turkey and stuffing, for chocolate mousse pie.

I cannot help it. This is how I see her.

And much later that night I see her again. But this time I am fast asleep. She appears, once again lit up, this time by the sun, for she is standing outdoors, in a field of sunflowers, against a paisley sky, and by her side is a sheep. And she is fat but she is pretty. She is smiling, tender shepherdess, and motioning with her right hand—making the same gesture over and over.

It struck me the next day when I remembered the way she had looked at me out of the dream: the gleam of urgency in her fine blue eyes, and the wafting gesture I now recognized as the same motion with which she had beckoned me into her home. My instinct was right, I felt it more strongly than ever. There was a reason Rouenna had got in touch with me. She wanted something.

※ ※

Stories happen only to people who can tell them: whoever said this was wrong. Nearer the truth is that favorite platitude of creative writing teachers: Anyone who has had a childhood has at least one novel in him.

Once, the editors of a literary journal sent me a questionnaire. Some kind of survey. Among other things they wanted to know: How in general do people respond when they hear that you have written a book? Give several examples if possible.

I never returned the questionnaire, but here are my answers.

1. I don't have time to read books.
2. Any chance your book will be made into a movie?
3. I wish I had time to write a book.
4. *My* life—now *that* would make a great book.

It was something new that I learned about people: how many of them believed their lives would make great books. My dentist and my hairdresser. The building super. Neighbors. The auditor sent by the IRS. And why not? They had all had childhoods. They had families; they had loved and been loved. The building super, shot and left for dead by government soldiers, had made a *harrowing* and *adventure-filled* escape from Guatemala to the United States. Stories—great stories—happen to everyone. And sometimes a person has a great story that he or she is dying to tell but has no ability to tell it. What then?

We were eating again, this time in an Indian restaurant around the corner from my building. It was my way of returning

Rouenna's hospitality, since I did not cook and, except for take-out, almost never ate at home (another habit of mine irritating to G.). A week after our big lunch, she called, as I had known she would. I wanted to avoid another trip to Brooklyn, so I invited her out to dinner. Anywhere is fine, she said, and I suggested the Indian restaurant.

Once more I was amazed at how little she ate, as if she had no appetite at all. Later I learned that in fact she never ate Indian food. She disliked spicy food. But she had been too shy, too polite or whatever, to say so. And when I learned this I could not help thinking, again, how different she was from other people I knew. I could not imagine any of my friends suffering in silence through a meal rather than asking to go to a different restaurant. (But then I could not think of any friend of mine who did not like spicy food.)

She did not eat, but she drank. She drank three Taj Mahals. And had it not been for all that nerve-giving brew, I might have had to wait longer to find out what it was she wanted. She wanted to write—she wanted me to help her write—a book about being an army nurse in Vietnam.

My guess was that this idea had not occurred to Rouenna until after she discovered my own book. She had come upon that book purely by chance. She was no reader, she confessed. "I don't have time to read books." (And yet she wanted to write one!) That day, on her lunch hour, she had gone to a bookstore, as she sometimes did, to browse through magazines. As she was leaving the store, she caught sight of my book. ("Your name jumped out at me.") The first book she had bought in as long as she could remember. She did not read. She did not even read books about Vietnam. (But perhaps this was not so surprising: another veteran, a student in a community college where I once taught, told me he had never read any book about the war—including the one I had assigned—and had likewise avoided all the movies.)

Rouenna bought my book that day, but it was more than a year before she read it. And though it was not a long book, it had taken her a long time—"weeks"—to finish it.

Unimaginable to me, this slow reading. But for those who did not read, who were not in the habit, this was how it must be. Take nothing for granted: recently I met a man, a graduate student of political science, who told me that he had never read a novel. He scratched his head at the very genre. "I mean, what is it exactly? What do you do—take things from real life? Make things up?"

So Rouenna, who did not read novels, who had not read any book in years, finally read this one book, mine, and was surprised. I had written about my past, which turned out to be part of her own past. You could do this, then. You could take things from the past, from real life, alter them, hammer a story out of them, share that story with the world. Possibilities that had never occurred to her before now presented themselves.

A great story had happened to her. There was just one problem.

I said no. I did not want to be cruel, but I had to be sure she understood. I would never write a book with or for someone else. I did not even suggest that she find another writer or try to write the book herself. I just wanted to discourage her.

And how easy she was to discourage. She gave up the idea just like that. She did not argue or try to change my mind. And I decided that after all it could not have meant so much to her. It was a fantasy, this idea of writing a memoir. It was the beer talking.

"I was just wondering," she said, and I blushed. So she had just been making conversation. She had not really expected me to say yes—it was I who had taken the idea too seriously. She was eating dessert, fried cheese with rosewater syrup, taking very small, delicate—I almost want to say *apologetic*—bites. And seeing her untroubled expression, I thought, So this wasn't it. This couldn't have been the thing she wanted from me.

Much fuss about the check. To my shock, Rouenna tried to pay it herself. Then she wanted to split it, and finally, when I reminded her that I was supposed to be taking her out, she insisted that I must not pay for the beer. The beer was too much, it should not be included, she had to pay for the beer herself. Again I thought: How different she is from everyone else.

I would remember this later, her insistence on paying for those three beers herself, and it would break my heart.

I began to see her regularly. I suppose it would not be inaccurate to say that we became friends, unlikely though friendship had seemed at first and different though this friendship was from all my other friendships.

She never brought up the subject of the book again, not even when we talked about Vietnam.

We met about once a month. We met for drinks or for dinner usually. Sometimes we met for lunch at a coffee shop near the store where she worked. I visited her apartment again a few times and invited her to mine. Twice we went together to the movies, and when autumn came we took a day trip upstate in Rouenna's car. This was her idea; it had been years, she said, since she had been to the country to see what she called "the coloring of the leaves." Later that year, in December, she took the vacation time she had coming to her and went to stay with her mother, who had been married and widowed twice again since Rouenna's father had died. For Christmas they flew together to Louisiana where Rouenna's brother had settled after marrying a woman from New Orleans and joining his in-laws' restaurant supply business. (There had been another brother, but he was long dead, killed on his motorcycle.) After the start of the new year, Rouenna and her mother returned to New Jersey. Rouenna still had a few days before she had to go back to work.

The past September my second book had come out, and in January I was invited to attend a writers' conference in San Francisco. A friend of mine insisted that while I was there I must look up an old friend of hers whose wife had recently left him. My friend thought I and this man might hit it off. I had been promised that he was handsome, and handsome he was, above all in profile, but I understood why his wife had left him. Such an air of broken dreams and resentment the man had. *This* handsome, his air seemed to say, and where has it got me. In that way, he reminded me of certain beautiful women. Just like a man, though, he made me feel as if I could never properly appreciate him. He made me feel harebrained. He made me feel small. A dry, mirthless laugh and dry cold hands . . . I agreed to go away with him for a weekend before flying home. The wine country. Why not? I was using him, of course; I was still a long way from being over G. And of course it went all wrong. Think of an old torch song: *His lips are sweet, but they are not your lips / His arms are strong, but oh—*

Whatever progress I had made getting over G. was reversed in those few short days. Not that they seemed so short to me . . .

Then—tragedy on the flight to New York: a man died in his seat. He was sitting across the aisle and just a few rows ahead of me. We never knew exactly what happened; we thought at first he was choking on something. The man had been traveling alone. The other passengers sitting in his row were bundled off into first class, though there were unoccupied seats in coach. The flight had about an hour to go. I thought someone would cover the man's face—say with one of those small blankets the flight attendants hand out with the pillows—but no. When the plane began its descent, one of the attendants checked to make sure the man's seat belt was fastened, but she did not cover his face. (Was this something done only in movies?) Getting off the plane, many of us had to file right past the body. People tried not to look.

When I got home, I found a message from Rouenna. She was still at her mother's, but she would be driving back to Brooklyn the next day, Sunday, and she wanted to make a date for some night that week. I replayed the message. Why, whenever she asked for something, did she always sound as if she expected to be told no? And why call from Jersey? Why not wait till she got home?

That breathy voice: always there seemed something urgent behind it.

Although she left her mother's number, I did not call Rouenna back. Instead, I left a message on her answering machine in Brooklyn. I said that I would be glad to see her any night that week.

And after I hung up I asked myself (and not for the first time, either): Why did I do that? Why did I go on seeing Rouenna? Once upon a time we had lived in the same neighborhood—was that so significant? What else did we have in common? If you had asked me whether I *enjoyed* seeing Rouenna, I would at least have hesitated before saying yes. I would never lose the feeling that she was after something. That I owed her, that knowing her might one day get me into trouble—against reason these feelings persisted. Seeing her almost always unsettled me. Seeing her at times depressed me. Yet none of this ever made me feel that I did not want to see her again. A part of me, at least, always looked forward to seeing her. But why?

She did not drive back that Sunday. Early Saturday morning snow began to fall. Saturday evening it was still coming down. It was very beautiful. I watched from my window, I watched my street fill up with snow. One of the few pieces of furniture I owned was a small maplewood rocking chair, and I had pulled this chair up to the window. The cat sat in my lap. While watching the snow and soothing the cat, who was always anxious after I had been away, I read. I was reading a very good book about a magical era in a snow-steeped Russia seen through the eyes of an ardent nostalgic young man. I was drinking hot cocoa. Earlier I had burned incense—not something I normally did, but someone had given me a packet of vanilla incense sticks for Christmas. So the air was tinged with those mingled scents, cocoa and vanilla. The cat had sat on the windowsill next to the incense as it burned; now the scent clung to his fur. Cats are said to hate this—strange scents on their fur—but this cat did not mind. It was only G. who minded when I tore those perfumed sample strips out of magazines and rubbed them down Southpaw's back.

Seen through the window from across the street, I thought how I must look: old. And I felt old, in my bare little room, in my rocking chair. Woman, cat, book. I had seen myself like this many times: it was my future. But in imagination it had always been my *distant* future . . . There were times when this image filled me with despair; other times it brought peace.

And right now I was at peace. After that grubby little affair in the wine country, after that man croaking on the plane, I was not unhappy to be home. (Though even as I read and watched the snow, I kept seeing them, out of the corner of each eye: the handsome man, the dead man: two profiles stamped on either side of the same coin.)

Meanwhile, in New Jersey, Rouenna was fixing something for herself and her mother to eat. She had cooked all that day and the day before—she had filled the refrigerator and the freezer with many small meals for her mother to heat in the microwave oven and eat after Rouenna was gone. I knew that Rouenna worried about her mother, who was in good health but, like many old people living alone, was not careful about what she ate. I knew also that Rouenna was weighing the possibility of moving in with her mother and commuting to work. Not a joyful prospect: Rouenna and her mother had never really got along. About her childhood Rouenna once said, "I was like Cinderella," and I knew what this meant: *I did all the housework and was unloved.*

And I guessed that it was partly to escape her family that Rouenna had joined the army: that time-honored responsible way to run away from home.

During this particular visit, besides all her cooking, Rouenna had taken her mother to the dentist and to the eye doctor and to talk to someone at her bank about some discrepancy in her checking account. She had gone through her mother's house, fixing this and that, turning mattresses, replacing washers, screwing new light bulbs into hard-to-reach sockets. Her vacation.

For supper that night there was chicken pot pie. After they finished eating, Rouenna washed up in the kitchen, then joined her mother in the living room to watch television. They watched an old melodrama about a man who is sent to jail for a murder actually committed by his best friend. Neither Rouenna nor her mother much liked the movie. Though neither mentioned it, the real murderer, the villain with his jutting brow and piercing raptor's gaze, reminded them both of Rouenna's father. Rouenna's mother fell asleep before the movie was half over. After a time she began to snore, and Rouenna, annoyed, roused her so that she could go to bed. Alone, Rouenna watched the movie to the end, and only then, seeing the real murderer shot through the heart by the wife of the wronged friend, did she remember that she had seen the movie before. Or perhaps it was just the ending she had seen. Now she turned to the Weather Channel. Snow and more snow. How would she drive back to Brooklyn tomorrow? Monday she had to be at work. Yawning, she watched the Weather Channel, learned what the skies were doing over the rest of the country and all over the world. She had a mild headache, she had had it all day. She turned off the television and sat a moment massaging her temples. Outside, the wind was rising.

In the bathroom, she opened the medicine cabinet and saw that her mother had never thrown out the heart medication that her last husband had been taking before he died. Though the expiration date had long passed, Rouenna knew that the medication was still good. It was still potent. She was a nurse. She knew exactly how many pills to take.

*

It is spring. The snow has melted. Rouenna has been dead for fourteen weeks. Soon after her death, I went away. Months earlier, in autumn, I had agreed to teach during the spring semester at a small private college in Massachusetts. Since I would be teaching only one class, and since that class met only once a week, on Wednesday mornings, I had planned to commute, taking the bus or the train on Tuesdays, staying the night in a bed-and-breakfast, and returning the next day right after class.

At the last minute I changed my mind. I arranged to rent a furnished apartment near the campus, and a week before the semester began I moved in.

Many years ago I heard about a couple who made plans to travel to Fiji—the most exotic place they could think of—the day after the funeral of their only child. I do not know whether this stratagem worked, but I understand the instinct that drove them. After Rouenna's death, one of the deepest feelings I knew was the desire to go away—much as I had felt after breaking up with G. New England was not Fiji, but it would do. Exotic to me, at least, this green valley, this genteel small town where smoking was forbidden even in the parks. Beautiful old houses, clean yards, conscientious recycling, a sign at the grocery store entrance announcing—as if it were a matter of goodwill and not the law—that shoppers of all colors and creeds were welcome. Exotic to me the wild turkey—bird I'd never seen, here seen often, in fields and backyards. Always the same flock, the one male (I called him G.) and the dozen drab females. Once, I saw him fan his tail and do a little swaying, stomping, feather-shaking dance, like a medicine man, while the wives huddled at a distance, discussing something else. When the snow melted, I came upon things I once knew but had all but forgotten. A robin's egg. A ladybug. Budding crocuses. Could I live here forever? Of course not. Yet this tidy, ordered small world and this simple teaching job would save me. The timing was so fortuitous, I could almost believe, as I have always so much wanted to believe, in a guardian angel.

Finding a place to live was not hard. The apartment, which is owned by the college, has two rooms, just like my apartment in the city, but these rooms are by comparison huge, nearly twice the size. Incredibly for small-town America, I do not need a car. It is a short walk to Main Street, a short walk to the campus, where, in a handsome old chapel, I have an office with enormous windows and a fine small library. As in the city, the new apartment is one of several carved out of what was once a roomy one-family house. My neighbors are other faculty members: one other writer and his family, the rest mostly women, a classics professor below me, a composer next door. These women are like me, about my age and single and living alone. If they weep I do not hear them.

The woman from the college rental office who showed me the apartment was clearly embarrassed: bare walls, bare floors, the absolute minimum of furniture. "I don't see why they can't do something to warm this place up." She kept shaking her head and apologizing. (I shook my head, too, but in wonder. *Fear of decoration.* Of course the angel would have known about that.)

There are mice. Southpaw is old, he is almost deaf, he is overfed, and the mice know this. Unlike the cat, I can hear them scratching in the walls at night, and in the morning I find what I think at first are dead ants on top of the stove and kitchen counters. Not good. But I am loath to set traps. Midsemester, I have to return to New York for a few days. I leave a box of spaghetti on the kitchen counter, and when I get back I find the box has been gnawed open and all the spaghetti is gone. A week later, cleaning house, I find the spaghetti neatly stacked like firewood behind the sofa. It is a cartoon that plays in my head for days: the mice stealing the spaghetti right under the nose of the snoring cat. (But how was it done? Did a mouse carry the spaghetti balanced crosswise in his mouth, or did two mice work together, one at each end?)

Such are my distractions. Here I am as solitary as I have ever been. At times I feel good about myself, I pat myself on the back: I am independent, I am stoic, I have few needs. I think of Pascal's saying that all our unhappiness comes from our inability to stay in our room alone, and feel smug. Other times I feel hopeless, worse than unloved, I feel the way I imagine an animal that has crawled off somewhere to die must feel. I am talking about moments of helpless misery, a drowning in pitch, a reckoning of failure and doom that is breathtaking.

Other distractions: this is academia, so plenty of turkey-cock-like stomping and feather-shaking—the usual bad manners, heavy drinking, gamesmanship, rivalry, back-biting, manipulation, paranoia, and seduction. I am lucky. Little of what goes on touches me. I am just passing through. I am just a visiting writer, and no one pays much attention to me. Besides, I have reached the age in a woman's life when to most eyes she is invisible.

January, February, March. In the period immediately following Rouenna's death, the idea that I had always had, the idea that had been there from the beginning, that there was something urgent between us, grew. It was something separate from the pain that thinking about her death brought me, but it was painful, too. It was painful, and it was painfully vague, and it cried out somehow to be expressed, yet seemed at the same time inexpressible. One of the first things I did was to buy a new notebook and write down everything I could remember about her. Though I had never had any interest in writing a book with her, I had always thought I might use something about her: her appearance, her apartment in Brooklyn, her howlers ("sometimes I think my finding your book that day was apocryphal"). The name Roro. What had happened in the Big Playground that day—this above all I thought I might use.

But the very first thing I did when I heard about her death was to call G. I could not help myself. I called him almost without thinking—it was pure need. But G. was purely baffled. "Wait—slow down a minute—*who* is this person?"

The question stung me like a whip. Of course, I had never told him about Rouenna. Most of my friends knew nothing of her. I had never introduced her to anyone. Whenever I thought about introducing her, I remembered what my friends were like. How critical they were, how snobbish. How no one was ever smart enough or attractive enough for them. How incurious they were about people who were not like them. How easily other people annoyed them. How often they said things like: He's boring, she's not very interesting, he's rather dull, she's not very bright. All meaning: He/she is not one of us. How they saw no reason to conceal their distaste for a person, not even from that person himself. Of course I must not introduce Rouenna to them—the sort of people she herself was so quick to lump together as *artistes*, so quick to condemn as *snotty*. Of course she would not fit in, and I had to protect her. (Or was it more myself I was concerned to protect, worried what people would think of me, for befriending someone like Rouenna?) So she was part of my secret life. It was almost like having an imaginary friend, the imaginary friend of childhood, or the familiar seen only by the eyes of insanity ("Have you met Harvey?"). Now, when I told friends what had happened, they were unmoved. Curious at last (suicides do tend to get their attention), but unmoved. I might as well have been inventing a crazy story. Many expressed astonishment that I had answered Rouenna's letter in the first place, much less agreed to see her. This infuriated me—but then I remembered what qualms I myself had had about meeting Rouenna, and how I was afraid of trouble.

And now I had trouble. Trouble working. Trouble not working. Trouble breathing in and out. News of her death broke all peace of mind, brought on headaches and insomnia. And all the while that feeling of urgency growing, intensifying, cutting off oxygen, pressing on my nerves. Pain. It was a good thing I was going away, a good thing I had a lot to take care of before the move. Throwing myself into these tasks brought some relief.

The first week—the week before classes began—was sunless and brutally cold. I did not go out much. I spent most of my time cleaning and arranging things in my new apartment and office. I went at this business with a fury, and when I was not at it I was restless, I did not know what to do with myself. There were moments when this restlessness waxed into anxiety and the anxiety into heart-pounding fear. In fact, it occurred to me one day that this banal formulation was perfectly apt, it described my situation exactly: I was living in fear. (And, as so often happens in such cases, after a while, since I was under no distinct, discernible, or even nameable threat, it would have been more accurate to say that I was living in fear of fear.) Now would have been the ideal time to be engaged in some large project: all this solitude, all these hours. As it was, I had just discarded the draft of a manuscript I had been working on for months. (How the word *discarded* bothers me—I want to say *destroyed* or, even more ceremoniously, *burned.* But when a writer says she burned her manuscript, suspect that she is not telling the truth. No one burns manuscripts anymore. Although once, in a cabin in New Hampshire where I'd gone to write, because I happened to have a fire going, I did burn a draft, page by slow page, and nothing was ever more hypnotically satisfying.)

So this was another factor in my decision to move: once again, I had gotten it into my head that in order to write I needed to be somewhere else.

I had brought with me the notebook in which I had written about Rouenna, and one day, after I had settled in, after I had arranged everything in the apartment and office and there was nothing left to be cleaned or put away, I sat down to read what I had written. It was not much. At the time, I had been too distraught to think or to write clearly—I was afraid to dwell on Rouenna then. So I started again. I quickly wrote down a description of how we met, and in the following days I kept it up—writing about other things I recalled from the time we'd spent together. I did not set aside a special hour of the day for this: instead I went about my life, and in the midst of doing one thing or another I would suddenly remember something and go write it down. And the more I wrote, the more I remembered, as always happens, and soon it had become a preoccupation. The feeling of urgency, again. But something had changed: I was less anxious. The fretfulness that had troubled me all these weeks diminished, and I relaxed. I slept better at night. My spirits lifted. I could breathe.

January, February, March, my birthday, spring. It was around the time of my birthday that I saw that, out of these notes and recollections about Rouenna, I might have begun a new book. I saw this partly because I was incapable of writing anything else; also because this writing was the only thing that could engage my full attention. A mother I knew once told me: When you have a child, if that child is not right there with you in the same room, you are never completely present yourself. Part of you is always elsewhere. I could have told her it was the same when you are writing a book. I went about my day, I did what I had to do, but whether it was reading or running errands or teaching class, my mind was never completely on these activities. Part of me was always elsewhere.

Other signs. I became not only calmer but also more aware. I began to notice things—the robin's egg that had fallen to the pavement, the ladybug on my windowsill, first the crocus, then the forsythia, and later the lilac—all things I might have missed or ignored before, all things that now touched me to the core, and stirred my imagination. The forsythia, especially, brought back my childhood. I remembered how, when I was in sixth grade and I began to show a tendency toward moments of excitability—the kind of overwrought state that inevitably ends in tears—alternating with moments of absence—daydreaming so deep I might have been sleepwalking—it was decided that I should be given some psychological tests. I remember only one result of these tests, largely because it became a big family joke. This particular test supposedly showed that, among occupations I might be suited for in later life, was that of—detective! I don't recall anything coming of all these tests (I was tested, then allowed to go to hell my own merry way), and I can't imagine that such tests are still in use today. But as I say, the notion of me as a detective struck the family funny bone, and I was teased about it for years. And for years I myself held on to the notion, for it is exciting to think that you might make a good detective, it is flattering. A bit of air was let out of the balloon when, home from my first year of college, I dated a police officer, a third-grade homicide detective with the NYPD, who laughed me and my little story to scorn: "Honey, you would not last one day."

There came a point when I decided that I could not proceed until I had got in touch with Rouenna's mother and asked her to send me a photograph.

Another time I went back through my date book and counted the exact number of times I had seen Rouenna, beginning with that first meeting in Brooklyn. Sixteen. Sixteen meetings of about two or three hours, a total of—what?—thirty-five to forty-five hours: not even two whole days. Plus our weekly telephone conversations, which might have lasted anywhere between five and thirty minutes. And suddenly I felt daunted: so much to remember, so much thinking to be done, so much I did not know, so much I could not bear to imagine.

Let it be said that I was not harboring any foolish idea that in writing about Rouenna I was bringing her back to life. I knew that even though I had gone away and crossed state lines, Rouenna was as dead in Massachusetts as she was in New York or in New Jersey. (I have always been haunted by an image of that poor couple weeping with a similar realization under the flawless blue skies of Fiji.) No: the one being brought back to life by this investigation was I.

It is spring. The snow has melted. Rouenna has been dead for fourteen weeks.

Soon, the semester will be over. But I think I can arrange to stay on a little longer, perhaps into the summer. I will stay on at least until the peonies bloom.

*

In the mid-fifties, a move from Brooklyn to Staten Island would have been seen as a move out of the city, to an almost rural world, without subways or high-rises, with forests, marshes, beaches, lakes, prairies, and even farmland. (Not too long before, much of Staten Island had indeed been farmland.) It was the opening of the Verrazano-Narrows Bridge that would change all this, dramatically and forever, but in the mid-fifties, when families such as Rouenna's and mine arrived on the north shore, that was still a good ten years off.

Some people said *in* Staten Island and others said *on* Staten Island, and no one seemed to know which was correct. *In* said Rouenna—it was one of the first things that struck me about her letter—and to me this has always sounded wrong. It jarred me, and it brought me back, her saying this—as did her saying "New York" when she meant Manhattan. "He works in New York," people would say, meaning he took the ferry from St. George across New York Bay to Manhattan. (In every school magazine, at least one lugubrious poem comparing commuters to souls being ferried to Hades.)

People called it the forgotten borough, the stepchild, or the Cinderella borough. "No one really lives there" is a very old New York joke. Sensitivity among the natives: "To them, we're just a place to dump garbage." Hostility toward City Hall, grumbling about taxes, talk of secession, of making separation from the metropolis not just psychological but real. A friendlier attitude toward New Jersey, to which many secessionists would rather belong. (And in fact, whether Staten Island belonged to New York or to New Jersey was a question hotly debated by the governors of those states for 150 years.) Weekend ritual: getting the kids into pajamas, tucking them in the back seat of the car, and heading over the kill to see a movie at the drive-in. (Eventually many would cross over for good; not just Rouenna's family and mine but scores of other people we knew ended up living somewhere in Jersey.) A shopper's paradise, with large outlet stores where you could buy both at a discount and without paying sales tax. In summer, day trips to the Shore or, for those better off, a week or a month in a rented bungalow. Capital of amusement parks. Asbury Park: Bruce Springsteen called it "Newark-by-the-beach." Summer dusk, bumper to bumper on the parkway, convertible top down, radio loud: "V-A-C-A-T-I-O-N!"

The rotten-egg stench of the refineries told you when you were almost home.

You could swim in the waters of Staten Island, too, but as the signs posted on the beaches warned, it was "at your own risk." People emerged from those waters streaked with tar, which they later tried to clean off with butter. You could have built a house with all the nail-studded wood that floated ashore (along with a mysteriously large number of green peppers).

Fort Wadsworth, the Lighthouse, the quaintly named Sailor's Snug Harbor—what sights Staten Island had to offer could be taken in in a day. "Many fine old churches and historic houses can still be seen." Early history lessons: *Staaten Eylandt,* Henry Hudson, Dutch settlers, 1661. School trips to old Richmondtown. "Oldest standing elementary schoolhouse in the country." To Tottenville, the southernmost tip of the state, to the site where, in 1776, John Adams, Benjamin Franklin, and Edward Rutledge sat down to claret and cold ham with His Majesty's Commissioner, Admiral William Lord Howe. "They met, they talked, they parted. And now, nothing remains but to fight it out." (Howe's secretary.) Our Founding Fathers, our history. Our heritage—nebulous, perhaps, to children of immigrants and postimmigrants, refugees from more recent wars, refugees from Jim Crow. How about the zoo with its renowned reptile house (world's largest collection of rattlesnakes) that were fed live prey before squealing audiences Sundays at three?

The lowest crime rate in the city. A good place to raise kids. A place that countless members of the NYPD liked to call home. Beloved of La Cosa Nostra. (To the list of sights add: the mansion atop Todt Hill, New York City's highest peak, where the godfather lived quietly with wife, mistress, and Dobermans, until he was gunned down outside Sparks Steak House in 1985.)

White neighborhoods, black neighborhoods. Don't get caught in the wrong place at the wrong (meaning any) time.

Note the large number of cemeteries. Note the number of institutions for the infirm, the disabled, and the unwanted. Some people who lived in the project worked at the Willowbrook State

School—among them Rouenna's father, who had a job there briefly as a groundskeeper. And I had a classmate who lived on those grounds; her father was an administrator. She told us stories . . . In 1972, when Geraldo Rivera sneaked in a camera and put those retarded children on the TV news, it seemed to taint us all. ("*Staten Island?* Isn't that where *Willowbrook* is?" Spoken in horror, as if you'd just said you were from the institution itself.)

A certain kind of person, a person with, say, certain artistic or intellectual or social ambitions, or a certain politics, would always feel a touch of chagrin about being from Staten Island. The largest trash heap in the world, *visible from outer space!* The provinces, the boonies, hicksville, no there there, and so on. Republican stronghold. Cultural backwater. So near Manhattan and yet so far! (What did you *do* there? people would ask me years later.) (And how many ambitious young Rastignacs have stood on the deck of the ferry boat gazing across the water at the beehive of Manhattan, tasting honey, hearts bursting with something like *A nous deux maintenant!*) I am talking about the kind of person who, years later, when Staten Island had been left far behind, would always reply to the question "Where are you from?" with "New York." ("The city?" "Yes.") But not Rouenna. Rouenna always said that she was from Staten Island. She often spoke of it as "the Island." ("In the Island," she would say, grating on my ear.) A British painter I know who worked for a time at Sailor's Snug Harbor, the "Home for Aged, Decrepit, and Worn-out Sailors" that in the eighties was turned into a cultural center, was amused by how local people always wanted first to know: Are you from the Island?

I like to think of Herman Melville coming often to Snug Harbor to visit its governor, his brother Tom. Maybe sitting down with some of the old salts to chat and reminisce about the sea.

Once you left, once you moved away, even if it was only to another part of New York, the name *Staten Island* seemed weirdly never to come up. You never seemed to meet anyone else who was from there, or who knew anyone from there, or who had ever even been there. Out-of-towners had only vaguely heard of it: Isn't that where the ferry goes? When it did come up, no one seemed to know anything about the place except for the famous landfill, Fresh Kills (or Not-So-Fresh Kills, as it was better known), and the famous children's institution. What about famous people? Well, Cornelius Vanderbilt was born on Staten Island and began his career as a boy, captaining one of the first ferry boats. His descendant Amy Vanderbilt was born and raised there, too, as were the photographer Alice Austen and the painter Jasper Francis Cropsey. Many more famous people have lived there: Frederick Law Olmsted had a farm on the south shore, and Henry David Thoreau lived with the Emersons of Emerson Hill, named after Judge William Emerson, brother of Ralph Waldo, who also sometimes lived there. Two poets, both Edwins, Edwin Arlington Robinson and Edwin Markham, and two sopranos, Jenny Lind and Eileen Farrell, the dancer Ruth St. Denis, the bank robber Willie Sutton, the great Barrymores—all lived somewhere sometime on Staten Island, as did Giuseppe Garibaldi, briefly, sharing a house with his countryman, the inventor Antonio Meucci. Anna Leonowens, the Anna who famously got to know the sixty-odd children of the king of Siam, lived in an area once owned by Daniel D. Tompkins, a governor of New York and U.S. vice president under James Monroe. Tompkins built one of the Island's first great hilltop mansions overlooking the harbor. Almost a hundred years later, S. I. New-house built his own Tudor mansion on a neighboring hill and, having just bought the *Staten Island Advance*, set about building his newspaper empire. All these people lived at one time or another in the forgotten borough, and let's not forget Maxim Gorky, Jane and Paul Bowles, and Dorothy Day.

Aaron Burr died on Staten Island, in an inn on the Kill Van Kull, not far from the site of our future home. The north shore: famous for shipbuilding during two world wars, and before that for oystering. Pollution put an end to the thriving oyster industry by 1916. By the time we arrived, almost nothing remained of old Captain's Row, where the fancy houses of rich oystermen once had stood.

Many tenants had put their names down for apartments in the Houses even before construction was finished. My parents signed up for five rooms on the top floor of one building sight unseen; they were already living in a low-income city housing project—how different could it be? Twenty-two buildings—twelve three stories and ten six stories—on twenty and a half acres—about six hundred apartments in all. We lived in a three-story building, and the Zycinskis lived across the street on the fourth floor of a six-story building. Only the taller buildings had elevators, and when the project started to go bad these were the buildings that went bad first. And even before those elevators were places where you could get hurt, they were places you wanted to avoid: the *stench*! Besides the Big Playground with its basketball court and adjacent softball field, there were several small playgrounds scattered through the project. The small playgrounds were for small kids, and the age when you were allowed to go to the Big Playground by yourself was a major milestone.

The ground floor of one of the six-story buildings held a recreation center and a laundry room. On Election Day, this was where you went to vote. Girl Scouts were assigned to keep an eye on the kids while their mothers were in the booths. When I was a Scout I had to do this, and if I sniff when I hear "JFK" it's because I am smelling bleach.

Outside the Houses, among people who lived in real houses—houses we would envy, no matter how humble they were—there was real dismay. Poor people had to live somewhere too: understood. But why in their neighborhood? Among outsiders there was a rule: Walk around the project and not through, no matter how much longer it takes. And it worked both ways. Once, about a mile from home, a group of us tried to run through someone's backyard. It was late, it was getting dark, we were looking for a shortcut. Out of nowhere, it seemed, three men appeared, two with bats. Oh so quietly we were told to go back where we belonged and stay there. And oh so quietly we went, the unspoken question pressing down on us with the gloaming: How did they know just by looking at us where we belonged?

One of the worst things about living in the project was its reputation among outsiders, who maligned it with tales of rapes and murders and other crimes that did not happen there, at least not then. The kinds of crime that happen there all the time now. No. What had Rouenna and me shaking our heads after all these years was not how dangerous a place the project was but how safe. Most people left their doors unlocked, at least during the day. There were no locks on the buildings and no window gates. There was a room in the basement of each building where you could keep bicycles and baby carriages, and though I recall some things taking place in those basements that should not have, I don't recall anything being stolen. Inside and out, the buildings were clean. There was no graffiti. In summer college students were hired to tend the grounds, and the sight of those tanned, crew-cut young men working shirtless in the sun could turn a young housewife's head (and they were all young, those house-wives then, some still in their teens). I don't suppose it occurred to any of us that it was a golden age we were living in, but it was. The project's age of innocence, its youth. Granted, not a place where you would choose to live if you didn't have to. When school friends declined your invitation to visit ("my parents won't let me"), when a cab driver at the ferry terminal refused to drive you home—this was bad, this was humiliating. But still. Better than most other low-income projects. Heaven on earth compared to where a lot of those tenants had lived before. ("Rats as long as your arm!") Not a ghetto. Not a slum. And yet like all housing projects, from the outset, by definition, as Jane Jacobs warned: *a mistake.*

The Zycinskis lived in their building just three years before moving to half of a duplex house down by the water, a stone's throw away. And from that day on the Zycinski children were warned to stay away from the project. *Walk around not through.* Us, we lived in the project fifteen years. Soon after I went away to college, my parents, all their children now grown, moved too. By this time the families we had known growing up were all gone. The turnover rate had gotten so high, some tenants moved in and out within the same year. Among those who had moved in when the Houses were new, only a handful remained.

From time to time the project made the newspapers—not just the *Advance* but *The New York Times* and the *Daily News.*

Today: "Every building a crack house." In a recent series of articles about housing projects in general, the *Times* reports that "fear of outsiders is deep." It was always deep. What business brought outsiders there? After I moved away, I heard this: To get into a certain fraternity, you had to walk through the Houses on a Saturday night alone. It was a brave thing to do.

To be attached to a place, to a certain house and landscape, a certain patch of ground—a place to which parents and grandparents have also been attached—what a strange thing this must be. What a wonderful thing, or so it has always seemed to me.

For me to go back to the project now would not be like going home, though it was my home for so many years. It was my whole childhood. But today it is another country, I am the outsider now, and I don't think I am brave enough to walk through those streets.

My first year away from home, I met a girl from upstate who grew up in a working-class neighborhood not far from a public housing project. "Easter Sunday after mass, we'd all pile in the car, roll up the windows and lock the doors, and drive through the project to gawk at the people in their Easter outfits."

"Why don't we take a drive there, you and me?" This was Rouenna speaking. "I mean, we got a right, we used to live there, it's not like we got no business there."

We'd get in her car and drive to the Brooklyn-Queens Expressway, we'd cross the Verrazano Bridge, get on the Staten Island Expressway and head west, then north on the Dr. Martin Luther King, Jr., Expressway.

"We'll stay in the car, we'll just drive through."

With the windows and the doors locked.

"And do what?" I said. "Gawk?"

She shrugged. "People gawk at me all the time."

I was taken aback. Was she talking about her weight? She was—I knew she was. And it was true, I had seen for myself how people sometimes stared at her, and I knew that she saw it, too.

I said, "I have a better idea. When was the last time you rode the ferry?"

But in the end it is I alone riding the ferry this bright cold day.

Late morning, a Monday, not many passengers. Mostly tourists. I hear German and French. The tourists stand with me on the outer deck before the boat leaves—*click click click*—but once we pull away from the dock, everyone hurries inside. "*Quel vent!*" Half an hour from now, when we have crossed the bay, these people will take the next boat straight back to Manhattan. It is only for the ride that they've come—no, not even for the ride; for the views. They will not be disappointed; it is cold but also sparkling clear. It was the strip of brilliant blue between window shade and window sash that I saw first thing on waking this morning that made me choose today for this little excursion. In thirty years I have been on the ferry just once before, thirteen years ago, when I was showing the sights to some friends from Brazil.

At the Manhattan terminal, after passing through the turnstile, I looked automatically to the left for the lunch counter where they used to serve the best frozen custard outside Coney Island. There was never a time coming home from the city that I did not treat myself to some, but not today. The lunch counter on the boat itself was known for its pretzels; I used to have mine with a cup of their oversweetened cola. But today I only remember the taste of these things. And I remember them well.

And I remember the bums, as much a part of the scene as the pigeons—some on a binge, some sleeping it off, some riding the boat, some wandering the terminal, especially on the Manhattan side: the Bowery isn't far. It seems to me there are more of these men now, as there are more homeless women. For years the same woman with hugely swollen legs sitting on the same bench of the terminal in St. George, Staten Island. Hands in lap, eyes on hands, silent except for an occasional remark to herself, utterly placid, as if she hadn't a need in the world. Scores of passengers streamed past her all day long. Had she looked up, she would have seen many of the same people over the years, she could have watched some of them grow: children first, holding on to their parents' hands; then loud teenagers, striking poses and dragging on cigarettes (permitted in the terminal and on the boat's lower deck in those days); then adults, commuting to work. But she never looked up from her lap, that woman. And for all she saw of those generations passing by, she might as well have been blind.

But if you looked, you could see some very interesting things in the ferry terminal. It was there that for the first time ever I saw real live women from India, women in saris, women with bindis. They might have been a flock of flamingos that had just landed beside us. *Stop staring!* my mother hissed.

Once the bridge and the expressway opened, the ferry became for many commuters the least desirable way to go. People preferred to drive or take a bus. There are people living on Staten Island now who have never taken the ferry. (There are people, it is said, who live on Staten Island their entire lives without ever leaving it—hard to believe, but not impossible. Still, try putting yourself into such a person's head—say someone living near enough to the shore to see, on a clear day such as this, the

Manhattan skyline. Imagine asking yourself: Why would I ever want to go there?)

For a time people were scared away from the ferry by a certain rowdy element, and many swore never to ride it again after the day a man went berserk and attacked several passengers with a sword. A police officer patrols the boat today—perhaps one of the many who live on the Island. Bored. Whistling. Rocking back on his heels and twirling his nightstick. Like a cop in a play.

I try to remember a poem I wrote when I was in school—one of those countless lugubrious efforts comparing commuters to souls being ferried to Hades. Instead I come up with Edna St. Vincent Millay's: *We were very tired, we were very merry— / We had gone back and forth all night on the ferry.* A love poem, at the end of which the lovers give all their money except their subway fare to some poor old woman. Yes, the ferry could be romantic, especially at night, especially in summer. I can remember such summer nights, being in love, being tired, being merry. I can remember riding the ferry at dawn in a long strapless dress, all bare collarbone and upswept hair, eating a cruller, pretending to be Audrey Hepburn in *Breakfast at Tiffany's.*

It was in summer, when school was out, that I went into the city most often, and mostly what I remember doing while riding the ferry was reading. (Often the place to which I was going back and forth was the Donnell Library.) Hence this association: Charlotte Brontë and the Statue of Liberty.

We are passing the Statue of Liberty when I recall not only *Jane Eyre* but also the shoeshine men. None working the boat today, but I can see them as clearly as I can the Japanese family sitting beside me. Wearing navy blue uniforms—shirts, trousers, peaked caps—and carrying wooden footrests and wooden boxes filled with brushes and rags and polish and wax, they walked up and down the boat, calling "Shine 'em! Shine 'em!"—a harsh deep growling call, so inhuman-sounding it made the children laugh, and trying to mimic it they burst out coughing. The men ignored them; they had business to do. Best business at rush hour, when it was so crowded many passengers had to stand the whole way.

These were not young men, the shoeshine men. Some I recall were stooped with age; one limped badly. And unlike the shoeshine men you saw all over Manhattan, on Shoeshine Row in Times Square, for example, those working the ferry were white. Why do I have it in my head that they were old seamen? Was it because they wore navy blue—because they worked on a boat? Was it this one's funny Popeye the Sailorman walk—that one's tattooed arms? Whoever—whatever—these men once had been, they were some of the oddest creatures I have ever seen. In the secret world where as a child I spent much of my time, they were trolls.

Mommy, where—
Stop staring!

Where did they live? Where did they sleep, where did they go at the end of the day? Wherever it was: no soap. Shoe polish had got in everywhere, not just in every pore of their hands but in the creases of their foreheads and the whorls of their ears. Everything was stained—skin, clothing—even their teeth.

Two men: one suited, sitting on a bench, his foot up on the footrest; the other man on his knees. The one man keeps reading, the wide pages of the *Times* or *The Wall Street Journal* like a screen between him and the other. A mystery: Why clean shoes that are already spotless? With incredible speed the shoeshine man works, unpacking rags and bottles and brushes and tins, then wiping, waxing, brushing, buffing. Why does no one else watch? It is fascinating. See how those hands move faster and faster—how on earth does he manage not to dirty the sock? Faster and faster—a matter of minutes—and now those shoes, which had seemed perfectly clean before, are simply dazzling, brighter than new, sleek and supple-looking, like licorice toffee.

In the time it takes the customer (who barely glances at his transformed feet) to dig into his pocket for change, the shoeshine man has repacked his box. But he does not get up, he waits on his knees until the coins have been dropped—from a safe height—into his blackened palm. And only then does he heave himself upright, wiping his brow—no wonder there is grime in the creases—and stump off in search of a new customer. "Shine 'em!"

Once, one of these trolls—the one who limped badly—came up to where I was sitting with my mother and wordlessly gave me a pack of Juicy Fruit gum.

I step outside. People have gathered on deck to see the Statue of Liberty, Ellis Island, and the Manhattan skyline. One couple has asked the policeman to take their picture with the skyline behind them. As he hands back the camera, he tells them to return at night "if you wanna see something *really* spectacular." Good tip. Right now it is so clear that you can make out the Brooklyn, Manhattan, and Williamsburg bridges. The water is choppy and dark. Cold. Forbidding. People wishing to die have jumped into that water; some have been saved and some have not. People have wished to have their ashes sprinkled from this spot. As always, there is much traffic: tugboats, motorboats, barges, tankers, vast container ships—islands unto themselves—a ferry going in the opposite direction. And beneath the busy surface lics another fleet—the ruins of old sailboats and steamboats and other vessels that have sunk over the years, some as long ago as a century. Bits and pieces from these hulks float in the harbor, along with all kinds of trash—flotsam and jetsam and then some. There are gulls in the air and gulls in the water—somehow they know to avoid the oil scum. Brown sludgy water that once teemed with shad and bass and other fish, and great variety of shellfish, including the famous oysters.

Another twenty minutes or so before we reach the place where the Upper New York Bay meets the Kill Van Kull, the channel separating Staten Island from New Jersey. The skylines of Jersey City, Newark, and Bayonne, and the arc of the Bayonne Bridge can all be seen from the ferry's starboard side. The view from port side is dominated by the colossus of the Verrazano bestriding the Narrows, its Island foot in Fort Wadsworth, whose first batteries were emplaced more than two hundred years ago to guard the harbor's entrance from invasion. And for some reason the thought that in all this time those guns have never been fired upon any invader and that the fort itself has been demilitarized and turned into a park—for some reason at this moment I find this incredibly moving.

Ahead lie the peaks and bluffs of Staten Island—those heights along the shore where, beginning at the turn of the century, the grandees built their villas and planted their gardens.

Our captain slows the boat and begins to steer it toward the landing slip at St. George. Before I was old enough to go to the Donnell, I used to come as far as St. George and use the public branch library there. Above St. George rises the hill where S. I. Newhouse lived. At the Manhattan terminal, before boarding the ferry, I bought a copy of the *Advance*, founded in 1886 and since 1922 a Newhouse publication.

It was Henry Hudson who named Staten Island, for the Dutch States General, and when in 1609 he went voyaging up the river that would be named for him, he took along two natives of the Island (to them it was Acquehonga Manacknong). Hostages. When the ship reached the place that is now West Point, they managed to jump overboard and escape. They were Raritans, a tribe of the Lenapes, who lived on the Island shores and penetrated inland mostly for hunting.

But the deer and the bear, the fox and the wolf did not long survive the arrival of the Europeans, and the hunting grounds were razed to make way for farms. Some historic trees remain from the days when the land was dense with locust, black walnut, and maple. Where once were colonial orchards, a few apple, plum, or cherry trees now stand. There are pockets of pastoral landscape—woods of hickory and oak, sweet gum, sassafras, and mulberry, surviving acres of salt meadow and marsh, swamps blooming with rose mallow and skunk cabbage. A grove of old-growth forest lives on the south shore, with ancient oak and beech and tulip trees. Nearby rise the primeval red clay ocean bluffs from where, on the clearest days, it is possible to see in one direction all the way to Manhattan and in the other all the way to Jersey's Atlantic Highlands.

Birds. On the beaches: gulls, cormorants, terns. In the wetlands: herons, egrets, ibis, grebes, kingfishers, ducks. In the woodlands: thrushes, warblers, scarlet tanagers, owls, woodpeckers, pheasants, hawks. And once a year, as summer bleeds into fall, the migrating monarch butterflies.

You might still be able to dig an oyster from these waters, but it would take a braver man even than Swift's to eat it. Oyster shells wash up on the sands, along with the shells of mussels and clams, horseshoe crabs, periwinkles, and whelks, which—when hung on the wall of her fisherman's cottage on the bay—looked to Dorothy Day "like false curls." It was in the mid-twenties—about the same time as Newhouse, though in a quite different style—that Day first came to live on Staten Island, not far from the place where she now lies buried. It was here that she became a Catholic. The natural beauty of her surroundings—so near Manhattan and yet so far—gave her great joy, as did riding the ferry boat—to her mind an ideal place for serious thinking.

The speed at which we go, neither too fast nor too slow, the boat's lulling rise and fall (echoed by some attendant gulls), the steady vibration of the engine felt to the bone, the crisp air pungent with salt and tar, the stately procession of bridges and skylines—all this is indeed conducive to thinking.

And I have been thinking and thinking—about Rouenna and how we had planned to ride the ferry together, but in the way of such things we never got around to it, the time was never quite right, the weather was not right, we forgot for a while, and then she was dead. And how I decided to do it alone, midsemester, when I had to return to New York on some business anyway, I would go down and ride the ferry one of those days, for Rouenna, for remembrance.

Thinking now also about something that Gregor von Rezzori wrote: *You must never undertake the search for time lost in the spirit of nostalgic tourism.* A warning. Pondering this as I gather with the tourists on the boat's bow—*click*—fascinated but forced to admit that I do not really understand what Gregor von Rezzori means.

Thinking about the policeman—*click*—not this one here among us waiting for the boat ramp to lower *click* but that other one, my summer romance, that last summer, my nineteenth, before I moved to Manhattan for good. How we rode the boat one sweltering midnight and how he kept talking (we were very tired, we were very drunk), there was something he wanted me to think about, to think really hard about, as he had been thinking, and I did think about it—cop's wife, couple of babies, Staten Island forever—and I said *Honey, I would not last one day.*

Slowly, the ramp comes down.

How can you remember so much? How do you keep it all in your head? Rouenna often asked me this. She herself had a bad memory, spoke of *black holes*—years of her life about which she could recall almost nothing. So she was often amazed at me: my perfectly average memory could seem prodigious to her. When we talked about the past, she would ask me questions. What was the name of that frizzy-red-haired woman who owned the candy store near school? What street was the Catholic church on? And so on. It thrilled her when I knew the answers.

Psychotherapy: as ordinary as moviegoing to my other friends, but to Rouenna foreign. How did people do it, sit down once or twice a week or even more often, week after week, sometimes for years, and talk about their pasts? How was that possible? How could there be so much to tell—how did they remember it all?

I tried to explain about the logic of memory, the mind like a many-roomed mansion, with doors opening from one room into another, and then another, but she cut me off: "I'll bet those people get most of it wrong." I tried to explain that, though probably true, ultimately this was not supposed to matter. She laughed at that. She laughed when I told her something a psychiatrist once told me: how many of his patients expressed the same fear, that somewhere, back in their pasts, a body lay buried.

"A *b-body*? *Whose* body? *What* body?"

Have I said that Rouenna had an odd laugh, a wheezing, sucking kind of laugh: she laughed backward, not out but in.

How much *does* it matter, what you remember, what you forget? Sometimes I think I want to be like that other kind of person, for whom it does not matter very much. One of those people who get on with life without ever looking back—for whom the past is like a great carpet that rolls up tightly behind you as you go.

Rouenna said, "I'll bet those people in therapy make half of it up."

After the end of the Vietnam War, some people got in touch with Rouenna. These were people who were doing research about the war, in some cases specifically about the women who had served. That they had gone to the effort to find her and wanted to hear her story took Rouenna by surprise. It had been years since she had come back from Vietnam. Then, she had been bursting with stories. Vietnam had been the first time in her life—it would be the only time, in fact—that she had done something out of the ordinary. Every minute of her tour she had been acutely aware of this—that she was experiencing things most people would never experience, seeing things most people would never see, things that others would have difficulty even believing when they heard—one incredible, sleepless year that would mark her forever and that nothing else in her life would ever live up to. But the timing was wrong. In the way of other returnees, Rouenna found that, whenever she brought up the war, people would change the subject or turn away. After a while she stopped telling people that she had even been to Vietnam— a thing she would not have believed possible while she was still there. And then, as the years passed and the wheel turned and the world decided it wanted to know what had happened over there after all—down to the smallest detail, as it often seemed—the timing was wrong again. Rouenna had changed, she no longer wanted to tell what happened. She had kept silent for so long, she had put that extraordinary year from her mind with such force, there were so many things she no longer remembered, so many black holes—"I told them the truth: Vietnam was the last thing I felt qualified to talk about."

In time, of course, the wheel would turn yet again, bringing the two of us together.

She did not talk to the people who wanted to interview her, she did not read the books or the articles that these people wrote. As for the many movies that began to appear: "Have you ever noticed in those movies how the actors are always too old for their roles?" I had. Just because you were old enough to be a soldier didn't mean you were old enough to play one. "Think of your high school yearbook, that's closer to the age most troopers really were. Some of them weren't even shaving yet. Then you have to see them the way I saw them, lying in all that pain, all that blood, and they look even younger. I swear, some of the dead ones looked about ten."

She had a calm, low-pitched way of talking about what she had seen. She was never emotional.

To serve in the war zone, an army nurse had to be at least twenty-one. Rouenna was twenty-two when she arrived in-country. Most of the combat troops were still in their teens. To a twenty-two-year-old woman, eighteen is *young*.

She did not talk about the war, she did not join any veterans' groups or participate in any veterans' events. Friends she had made during the war—for life, they had sworn—she could not tell you where they were today. By 1982, the year of the dedication of the Vietnam Veterans Memorial in Washington, D.C., the army, Vietnam, nursing itself were all more than a decade behind her. ("Another life.") But all through the eighties people continued to get in touch with her, among them other women veterans who had decided the time had come for them to speak. To Rouenna, it was bewildering. Why now—why not all those years back when the memories were still fresh? And she wondered about all those stories. Too much time had passed, and she was skeptical. All those perfect memories—who could trust them? ("I'll bet those people make half of it up.") Don't tell her she was the only one who had a problem with black holes. She said, "There are a lot of liars out there." And she told this story. After her discharge from the army, she had worked for a while in a public hospital, and she was shocked at the number of drifters who passed through claiming to have fought in Vietnam. "I asked one of them where he was stationed in-country, and believe it or not the bum said Hanoi! Too bad for him I happened right then to be drawing blood—I jabbed that needle pretty rough into his arm."

It isn't true that she was *never* emotional.

Though she had seen her share of combat fatigue ("all we could do for those guys was knock them out and let them sleep sleep sleep"), she never knew quite what to make of all those cases of what came to be called post-traumatic stress disorder. "One vet I know told me his therapist said he probably had PTSD before he ever even set foot in Vietnam. Now, what is that supposed to mean? How can it be *post* if it was there *before*? Then this therapist tells him the only cure is to talk about the war as much as possible, get it all out. So he does, and then he goes back to her and says, Now can you tell me how to get my wife and friends back?" A variation on an old shrink joke, but Rouenna did not seem to know this. (Even so, when she told this story, she laughed hard, as at a good joke.)

She said, "They should have stuck to calling it combat fatigue. PTSD sounds like some kind of bug juice." Another equally ugly new name for it during the war was "acute environmental reaction." The further back in time, the more lyrical the name. *Shell shock* before *combat fatigue*, and before that *soldier's heart*.

She said, "You know poetry, right?" And before I could even think how to reply, she had rattled off the whole of "Stopping by Woods on a Snowy Evening." Well. Where did *that* come from? Had she memorized the poem in school? She shook her head. She was excited—almost breathless. And she told this story. There was this little guy (further proof of how young those soldiers looked to her: she was forever referring to this or that "little guy," as if platoons of dwarves had fought over there) from New Hampshire—"or maybe it was Vermont—somewhere up there." Somewhere this little guy was never going to see again. "We knew it and he knew it, he didn't have much time, there was nothing we could do for him and all he wanted was for someone to read to him from this paperback he carried with him, this book of poems. Toward the end it was just the one poem he wanted to hear, over and over. We didn't know what it was about that one poem that meant so much to him." Though now and then over the years a scrap of the poem might float into her head, this was the first time it had come flooding back in its entirety, and it was this that had taken her breath away. "Now you know if I had *tried* to remember it, it would never have come." We sat a few moments in appreciative silence. By this time I knew that this lover of Frost would have been known as an "expectant" and would have been placed behind a screen or a curtain in a special area with others expected to die. I wondered whether longer ago there might have been a more poetical word for this, too.

Rouenna said, "He was a sweetie. You got ones like that, kids who knew they were going to die and just wanted to die quietly, without giving too much trouble. But some of those guys? Let me tell you, if they're having nightmares thirty years later, believe me they *earned* it. You would not believe some of the sick things—you know about the souvenirs, right?"

One of Rouenna's favorite remarks was "I got no use for that kind of person." She herself was the kind of person other people used to describe as "one tough broad." The phrase came to me often when I listened to her talk. When she said "I never cry," I knew she was telling the truth.

"Finding your book. For me that was the apocryphal moment. Reading about the projects and having things start to come back." Things from her own childhood, she meant. "I could remember some things and not other things, and I wasn't sure if what I remembered was really how it was or if I'd got it all wrong. I couldn't say for sure that *anything* I remembered was accurate. When I thought about Vietnam, though that was closer in time, it was even worse." A helicopter gunner called Grub. "That's it—that's all I can tell you. Not his real name or where he was from or whatever happened to him. Not his face, not the color of his eyes or his hair. Just 'Grub'—and the fact that we had sex about one hundred times."

When the need to remember came, it was not without embarrassment. "I don't want to sound like some wimp." *Wimp* was another favorite word. A wimp was the kind of person who, instead of getting on with life, would rather "whine about the war." She had no use for that kind of person. All this to suggest how conflicted she was, which surely helps to explain why, when I refused to encourage her idea of writing about the war, she had no trouble burying it completely again.

Was it true what I had heard—that many of the women who served in Vietnam later experienced the same problems as male veterans, and that many of them had also been diagnosed with PTSD?

Rouenna was firm. "One thing I can say for sure: I never had no PTSD."

So: no nightmares, no flashbacks, depressions, anxiety, or insomnia, no panic attacks, rage attacks, suicidal thoughts, homicidal thoughts—

Oh, well sure, of course. At some point or other.

What?

All that.

And she never thought about seeking help from a therapist?

No way! She laughed her funny backward laugh. "And in my case, you know, those are *real* bodies buried back there."

When I finally asked her why she didn't sit down and write the book herself, the answer she gave was not the one I expected.

"I figured if I got someone else involved, it would keep me honest. Because my fear is not only that I would get things wrong, but that I'd be tempted to make things up, and then what?"

My turn to laugh. "Then you'd have a novel."

The logic of memory, one room opening into another room, one recollection leading to another. First this happened, then that. And to fill the gaps, the logic of imagination: this is the way it must have been. Stepping off the ferry boat, onto Staten Island, entering the terminal, I think of that woman with the swollen legs, and remember the nun. She too sat hour upon hour in this place, a tin plate on her knees, wearing the medieval-looking habit that you don't see many nuns wearing anymore. From time to time lifting the plate with its few coins and giving it a light shake. She had a broad pale ageless face. Strange, how it never changed expression. My mother used the word *simpleton.* But I saw something else. Class trip to the city, the Metropolitan Museum of Art. The nun is everywhere. Hearkening to the Angel, dandling her Child, kneeling at the foot of the Cross. Her broad pale changeless wimpled face. A dime ringing on a counter can bring it back; a tambourine, gently shaken.

I look for what I remember—the nun, the flower stand, the pastry shop—all gone. Only the newsstand is familiar. I am talking about the area outside the terminal, where the air smells of exhaust from all the buses waiting to take you along various Island routes. The numbers of these bus routes have been changed since I used to ride them. Still, I know which ramp to mount for the one that would take me—home. A few years ago I told a friend that I wanted to go back to the project sometime but that I was hesitant to do it alone. I was touched when she offered to go with me. Then she laughed and said, "Just give me time to get my shots."

Wandering the terminal, I miss the boat that left just after we arrived, the one that all the tourists, informed by their guide-books that there was nothing on Staten Island worth a detour, boarded; now it is a half-hour wait till the next. I wander the terminal, feeling a little absurd. What is there to see? Post office, photo lab, delicatessen. The waiting room is empty, but over the next half-hour it will slowly fill. A sordid place, with trash cans overflowing onto the floor. A sweet-and-sour odor. Rot. Braver souls than I visit the restrooms. Midday—so what are people doing asleep? Take this fellow with his shirt thrown over his head, as if this were an airport where he'd been delayed overnight. And *here* is a shoeshine man, sitting on a crate beside his vacant shoeshine throne. No customers, nothing to do but clap away the pigeons that have managed to get trapped indoors and strut about pecking at imaginary seeds in the linoleum. Unlike the shoeshine man, the fast-food servers are doing a good business—it seems at least half the people waiting are eating something wrapped in greasy paper. A family—mother, father, boy—lunching on french fries and doughnuts. Some-thing about the way the boy eats annoys the father, who smacks him upside the head. The startled boy lets the doughnut fall to the floor. He wails. The father curses and kicks the doughnut in the direction of a trash can, and instantly all the pigeons are on it. As they tear it apart, the shoeshine man starts up a rhythmic clapping, the sound loud in this cavernous place. The boy raises his wail, the father hits him again, the mother watches—the whole time she has never stopped eating. No one else pays attention. Those who are not truly asleep are sleepwalking in the perfected big-city-dweller's way: able to go about business while remaining unconscious.

This is an ugly ugly place. Something in me wants to say it out loud. I do not remember it always being so grim. Something in me wants to shout, get an echo going in this cavernous place. *Why* so ugly? Why so *grim grim grim?*

So when the boat finally comes, it is a relief. But all the way riding back, I am uneasy. I have a feeling of unfinished business and am reminded of one of those dreams in which you set out on some mission and after countless distractions and obstacles are just about to accomplish the thing when of course you wake up. Nothing you would not give to be able to go back . . . Probably there is a name for this feeling, but I don't know it. I march up and down the decks, the nameless feeling grows and grows, and by the time we reach Manhattan it has become an agony of restlessness. Impossible to return to my apartment. I get on the subway and ride to Union Square. I change trains, and minutes later I am in Brooklyn.

I have not eaten yet today, so I go first to one of the small Polish restaurants and order some potato pancakes. I have been here a few times, both with Rouenna and also before I knew her. I sit at a table near the front from where I can see the street. Much has been said of the art-world uniform, and here in this neighborhood—and this must be a first—you can tell the artists from the natives because the artists are so much better dressed.

For it is chic, the art-world uniform, and those I see passing by are mostly young, or young looking, people with style, male and female both, people who take care of themselves. I see marvelous haircuts, marvelous shoes.

How long before I see someone I know? I used to worry about this whenever I was with Rouenna. Rouenna, who watched the same uniformed parade with a scowl. "Look at them all, in their little chi-chi black outfits and punk hair. God, I wish they would move somewhere else." Actually, she wished they would die. (Never again would I wear a certain little black outfit of my own after she looked me up and down and said, "All you need is some Ho Chi Minh sandals and an AK-47.")

A water main broke in Herald Square, and the store where Rouenna worked was flooded. That was *her* reason for being home on a weekday, but what about everyone else? Didn't any of these people work? Where did they get their money? Rouenna was sure that they all had trust funds. Though I know this isn't true, sometimes I too have to wonder. The clothes, the hair, the lofts (the days when rents in this neighborhood were cheap are long gone), the almost nightly dining out, the yoga and tai chi classes, the therapy. The freedom—time and money to travel, to visit Berlin or Rome for a month, to spend two months at an art colony—how do they do it? These are hard times for artists, after all—only a handful of them are living off the sale of their work. The rest are struggling, as artists have always struggled, but the signs of that struggle remain miraculously hidden. To Rouenna I suggested that a lot of them probably worked at night. But of course this was a lie. I know the hot little bars and clubs, here and in downtown Manhattan, where night will find them. This is a world I know pretty well. This is G.'s world.

Once, in this same street but in a different restaurant, sitting again at a table by the window, not alone but with Rouenna, I saw someone I did not know but whom I recognized from photographs: Maya Lin. I pointed her out. Blank look. I shook my head in disbelief. "The woman who designed the Wall?" Rouenna caught just a glimpse of her as she passed. Her blue eyes widened. Her turn for disbelief. "You mean they got a gook to do that?"

While I am having coffee, I take out the newspaper I bought at the ferry terminal and skim the lead article. The perennial issue of the landfill. The damage it has done to Staten Island's reputation . . . the cancers it might be responsible for . . . will the city keep its promise to close it for good early in the new century.

By the time I have paid the check, though less restless than before, I am still not ready to go home. So I walk—more or less the same walk I took the day I first came to visit Rouenna.

You can taste something, and that taste can wake memories of a time when you tasted that same thing before. But the reverse also can happen, and it is happening to me now as I walk along, the taste of chocolate mousse in my mouth.

The sign posted by the woman looking for someone to share her loft is gone. The Polish-joke graffito remains, indelible.

Rouenna's building looks, in spite of everything, the same. From across the street I see that the windows of the apartment where she lived (who lives there now?) are closed. But the old woman on the ground floor has hers open, she has her old yellowish-gray head out, and as I approach she astounds me by calling "Oh hello, dearie, how are ya?" as if she knew me. She does know who I am, for she says next, "Ain't it a shame about

Roseanna?" *Rouenna*, I correct her, but she pretends not to hear. Or more likely she really does not hear. She is old. She has a cancer on her nose, a cataract on her eye—why not also something obstructing her ear?

She could tell me: Is there a new tenant in Rouenna's apartment? The question appears to shock her. She thinks I want the apartment for myself. She thinks that is why I have come. Or so I take it from her dirty look, the way she ducks her head back inside and lowers the window without a word. But who knows. She is old. She is feeble-minded. *Barely able to take care of herself*, wasn't that how she was described? Who brings her leftover turkey, now that "Roseanna" is gone?

As I move off down the street, a sparrow hops in my path, and I remember the parakeets. *What happened to Romeo and Juliet?*

I am tired. I drag my feet walking back to the train station. I think with dread about this evening and its obligatory event: a book party. It is this that has brought me down from Massachusetts. But the party is not for hours yet. There is still time—there is still one more stop I want to make.

Back at Union Square, I change trains again and ride up to Thirty-fourth Street—the same way Rouenna went to her job every day. I have never been inside the store where she worked. I know that it is part of a chain that sells clothes exclusively for women sizes twelve and up. I have seen their ad: THIS IS WHAT A SIZE TWELVE LOOKS LIKE, with a picture of Marilyn Monroe. The famous full-length portrait, taken from the back, white bathing suit, high heels, looking over her shoulder. I know about the chain's policy of hiring only saleswomen who wear plus sizes themselves—and I know about the very strange (size four) woman somewhere in the Midwest who is suing the company that owns the chain, for job discrimination. ("I sure would like to go find that skinny bitch and kick her skinny butt," Rouenna said. "I got no use what-so-ever for that kind of person.") Rouenna, size eighteen, had been a saleswoman (and a size sixteen) before she became a manager. She had been happy at the store, partly because working there had so neatly simplified her life. Able to choose clothes from a huge selection and buy them at an employee discount, Rouenna, who hated clothes shopping, now never needed to look anywhere else. The store stocked even extra-large hosiery and underwear, and special, hard-to-find leather gloves, for small plump hands (Rouenna's were like two whole chicken breasts).

No mannequins in the windows, just different arrangements of the clothes themselves draped or hanging there—the long loose dresses and tunics and wide pants with elastic or drawstrings at the waist that I had come to associate with Rouenna and the sight of which now, in all their ghostly emptiness, brings a pang. It is past the lunch hour, and there are few customers. A security guard dozes on a stool by the door. Monroe beams gigantic down from one wall. Things change. That is not what a size twelve looks like anymore. A saleswoman approaches, carrying what I guess to be close to two hundred pounds, but with dignity. She is very tall—*statuesque* was the word invented for her—and her knee-length skirt reveals shapely legs. I have to stop myself from shaking my head when I see that she is wearing spike heels: all that weight and a job that requires you to stand all day. Yet she hardly looks uncomfortable. Another mystery: How does she work with those fingernails? (I once heard someone on line at a supermarket ask the cashier, who had nails like the emperor of China, "How do you scratch your ass?")

My intention was to walk in the store, have a quick look around, and leave. But when this woman asks if I need any help, I find myself blurting the truth. I tell her I wanted to see where my friend used to work. "Oh," she says, carefully interlacing her fingers. "That was so sad." Another saleswoman standing nearby overhears us, walks over, and adds, "We all felt so sad." We stand there, the three of us, looking at one another, stones on our tongues, until we are joined by a fourth woman, who turns out to be the new manager. I want to ask these women questions—if only I knew what the questions were. Unprompted, the women say the kind of thing people always say about the dead. Rouenna was a good person. Rouenna would be missed. They tell me it was a shock when they heard about her death. They had not noticed anything unusual about Rouenna, she had not seemed particularly troubled or depressed before she went on vacation. No. They are sympathetic, these women, but their eyes are dry. It is clear that they did not know Rouenna well, they were not close to her, they have not really thought much about her since her death, or at least that is how it seems to me. The minutes lengthen and grow weighty. The women shift from high-heeled foot to high-heeled foot, examining their extraordinary not-for-ass-scratching nails, and I think how Rouenna would not have fit in with them. She did not wear such shoes, she did not have such nails, and she was older than these women, by many years—by a generation, as I am. Also, large though all three of them are, Rouenna was larger still. Some customers have come in now, and the manager is looking antsy, as if she thinks enough time has been wasted and they should all get back to work. So I gather myself to go. For some reason my heart is pounding. "I'll bet none of you knew that she was a combat nurse. I'll bet you didn't know that she was in the army, she was a lieutenant in the U.S. Army, did you. I'll bet you didn't know that she served in Vietnam." All this comes out much louder than intended—loud enough to wake the security guard dozing on his stool. The women stand rigid, staring at me, and seeing the expressions on their fat faces I feel a tiny swell of satisfaction. It is fleeting, though, indeed already gone, replaced with a more familiar hollow feeling, by the time I have passed through the door.

*

After I got out of college, I had a job as a secretary at a magazine. There, at the magazine's office in midtown Manhattan, I met a British journalist who happened to be living that year in New York—he had a teaching job at Columbia. At that time I was living near the university, and we turned out to be neighbors in the same street. After we met at the office—he was there to see one of the editors, he was writing an article—we ran into each other several times, and then we began to meet by arrangement.

A broken man. That is what he was, as I would understand later, but at the time I would never have used such a word to describe him. *Virile* is a word I did actually use to describe him, to my roommates, embarrassing now to confess. Later I saw what I was too young—too smitten—to see then: a wreck of a man, aged before his time, a man in pieces, never to be whole again. Not handsome—you could not call him handsome—but attractive—I think most people would have given him that. In his early forties but looking much older—only more handsomely so to my

twenty-two-year-old mind. Deep lines—real gashes—in his forehead and cheeks. Thin gray hair. Eyes also gray—blue-gray—
eyes of extraordinary sharpness. Intelligence: not every bright
person looks it, but his was the most intelligent face I have ever
seen. Further to beguile me: a love of words, a keen memory, a
memory for detail, a gift for anecdote. More than anything I
liked to hear him talk, and, unlike other men I had known up till
then, he liked to talk, and in 1973 what he liked to talk about
most was Vietnam. All the more riveting because through college
I had been dating an ex-GI who, though active in Vietnam Veterans Against the War, never had a conversation with me about his
time over there, not one.

But when I say my journalist talked about Vietnam, I don't
mean he talked just about the war. For him, Vietnam was the
name of a country first. As a correspondent, he had been there
many times, the first time in the fifties—"before most Americans
ever even heard of it." Always he had loved it, and now he was
"in a state of mourning for it." Something here was over my
head. I didn't understand the love he described, I thought there
had to be more to it, more than he was telling me, more perhaps
than he himself knew. He had a wife at home, in England. True,
they were separated, but still—was it not strange?—he seemed
to miss Vietnam more than he missed England, and to miss
people he had known in Vietnam more than he missed his
English wife, family, friends. For what they had done to this land
he so loved, he hated the French and the Americans, but he
hated the Communists, too. Admiration for Ho Chi Minh and
General Giap aside, he believed a Communist victory, which he
predicted any day, would bring disasters as cruel as the disasters
of war.

I would understand everything better, he once said, if I read his favorite book, which I did immediately, and so for a time *The Quiet American* was my favorite book, too.

Vietnam, North and South—he had traveled it up and down before the devastation wrought by bombing and defoliation missions, and it was a land of great green beauty that he painted for me. Place names he pronounced somewhat differently from the way I was used to hearing them—and the way he talked about Vietnam, he might have been talking about Italy or France, a place any sane person would want to visit or, better still, live: gorgeous scenery, fascinating people, great food. Strange to hear anyone rhapsodize over the fabulous French restaurants of Nha Trang. ("Oh, the lobster! The champagne!") He spoke also of places whose names were more familiar to me, the Continental and the Caravelle and the Majestic—hotels in Saigon where foreign correspondents stayed. But when he told me about gathering on hotel roofs at the end of a day, for cocktails—and a panoramic view of tracers and mortar bursts—he might as well have been talking about martinis on the moon.

Yes, my image of Saigon as hell—filthy, chaotic, corrupt, unsafe—was accurate, but: "Think of white villas, green palms, sampans floating on blue water." The Paris of the Orient—much of it destroyed during the Tet offensive—had Parisian-style avenues lined with trees, a river, bridges and parks, a botanical garden, a Chinatown, a zoo. He had liked visiting the Saigon zoo. He liked animals, and the animals of Vietnam—even for these least he grieved: the chickens, ducks, and pigs routinely slaughtered in the routine destruction of villages; the water buffalo blown up by mines; tigers and elephants and monkeys and birds (some very rare) caught in the B-52 and herbicide raids; the zoo residents, wounded, starving, forced to devour their own mates. A terrible story about some napalmed creature—I forget now what it was—appearing suddenly, somewhere—"no one could get to it" (curfew, snipers)—taking forever to die.

Over the years he had made friends with many Vietnamese, some of whom he had kept in touch with and hoped to see again. About those he had lost touch with he was always very anxious. He was anxious about the fate of all the people, even those he did not know. A friendly, stoical people, he described the Vietnamese to me, big on family ties, in general cheerful and brave. It amazed him how many of those he knew had managed to remain cheerful and brave in spite of all they had been through. (Not a single family he knew without its war victim; when a Vietnamese was drafted into the army, it was assumed he would not be coming home.) For him, such stoicism was a sign of innate Vietnamese worth. (He had no trouble at all with the notion that some races were innately worthier than others.) Among the Americans, he said, was a saying you heard all the time over there (we heard it also over here): One American soldier was the equal of two or three dinks. But in his view it was the other way around, and he thought any Vietnamese was worth a dozen Americans. ("Hell of a lot better looking, too.") Most of his experience of Americans so far had been those in the military and in academia, and between the two groups he had formed a mighty low opinion of us. He had had a hard time being around American troops. On Saigon's Tu Do Street he had watched a GI grab a pickpocket of about six or seven and slowly, deliberately—and to the wild cheers of his pals—snap all ten of the child's fingers, his wrists, and his arms. (I did not ask why, if it was done so slowly, he had not tried to intervene.)

He had more horror stories like this to tell, but most of his stories were about the other Vietnam. Mysterious, beautiful, it rose before my dazzled eyes: highlands, jungle, beach. Land of spectacular sunrises and even more spectacular sunsets. Land of the smiling and brave. Round friendly faces under triangular hats. Loving families working together in tender green paddies, rhythmically stooping and rising. Hard work, light hearts, bright laughter under bright sun . . .

These stories gave birth to the most intense romantic yearning in me.

The two of us, eating lobster, drinking champagne, in a restaurant overlooking the South China Sea. I could imagine it one day, he could not. To begin with, most of those restaurants had been blown up. Oh, the war would end all right, and soon. But the New Vietnam would be no place for tourists—at least not for a very long time. Probably not in our lifetimes, he thought. Wrong! Not even a generation, after all. I would not call that a very long time. For me those years went by in an eye-blink . . .

Wrong, but not wrong, since he himself would not survive those years.

In the beginning we spent a lot of time on the phone—far more time talking on the phone than seeing each other. To remember that voice is to remember two sounds that always accompanied it: matches being struck, ice clinking in a glass. Whole packs of cigarettes, whole bottles of whiskey were consumed during those conversations. (At my end it was cigarettes and diet soda.) Often we talked late into the night—once, all through the night. I remember replacing the receiver and hearing the birds in Riverside Park and how, when I turned off the bedside lamp, the room stayed light. I remember lying in bed, watching the room fill up with sun, exhausted but unable to sleep—head too full of mad Vietnam honeymoon fantasies (lobster and champagne and the South China Sea)—and how I finally admitted to myself that I was falling in love with a man twice my age, married, who hated Americans, and who was not in love with me, and the tears that kept running into my ears and back out my eyes—my downstairs neighbor getting up, putting Roberta Flack ("Killing Me Softly") on the stereo—were for all the suffering that I knew was coming to me. For though I had not yet dined in any fabulous French restaurants, I had seen quite a few French movies.

We met in winter. When we got together, if the weather was not too windy or cold, we would walk around the campus or through the park. He did not like the neighborhood hangouts, too full of students—he didn't like being around college kids. Something about their youth, their rowdiness when they'd had a beer or two, their loudness, and above all their language—*Fucking dude was wrecked out of his motherfucking mind, man!*—brought back the hated GIs. We avoided each other's apartments, too. I was too shy to invite him to mine—it was like a dorm suite—I had three roommates and little privacy. And he—I guess he was trying to be good. Came spring semester. *(Spring!)* Soon he would be gone.

A new urgency about those phone calls, harder and harder to say good-bye, each time a reminder of the big one to come ("Every time we say good-bye . . ."). Every time, dying a little.

We began to meet every day.

L'heure bleue in Riverside Park. We have watched the sun dissolve in the Hudson. First kiss. A deep one. Dying a lot.

The face I love looks even older in natural light, the gashes deeper, the hair almost white. The eyes as sharp and intelligent as ever, but bloodshot, ever bloodshot.

What—are you cold?

No, not cold. Unsayable premonition.

One night, after talking for hours on the phone, we sigh and hang up. I have just gone to bed when the phone rings again. Forgive me I need you can't help it won't you come to me. The voice I love is trembling. *And I all trembling too leap up and slip into coat and boots run down stairs down dark street his building then up stairs his door throw coat off now naked except boots his arms oh his arms—*

When it was down to a matter of two weeks, I moved in with him. It was the state of that apartment that fully alerted me. The squalor of those rooms. The many empty bottles. The empty *broken* bottles. In Saigon, he said, he had been a much-too-frequent visitor to an opium house in Cholon, the Chinese quarter, but he had been cured by an acupuncturist he discovered just a few doors down from the opium house. Now his only drug was pot. He smoked a little every day, usually early in the day, and after a certain hour he switched to drink.

Stupor of drink, stupor of despair—don't ask me where one left off and the other began. I knew he was in deep. Love could not blind me completely to that. Most days he seemed hardly to know what to do with himself. He was supposed to be writing a book—parts of it were published in the magazine—but he did little writing that year, and in fact he would never finish a book—

any book. He had taken the teaching job more or less out of desperation. Things had somehow gone wrong between him and the editor of his paper, he wanted to be away from England, and he needed the money. I sat in on some of his classes and, in spite of his great gift for storytelling, at the lectern he fumbled, he droned. I saw some of the students exchange smirks, and my face burned for him.

Acupuncture had not cured him. He died a few years later from a heroin overdose that some said was only made to look accidental.

By that time we were out of touch—in fact, despite all the heavy breathless promises of those final two weeks, I never heard from him after we parted, not one line.

Immediately after he left for England, a woman who was an editor at the magazine took me aside: He and his wife were not *really* separated.

I heard also that at the time of his death he was writing a memoir about Vietnam. I believe he managed to go back there one last time, but I'm not sure. I hope he did.

The Quiet American. I read it because he wanted me to, and when I did I thought I had found if not the answer at least a large clue to the mystery.

Thomas Fowler, British reporter in Vietnam, anti-American, estranged from his wife, afflicted with melancholy, smoker of opium—well, there was just one parallel missing, it seemed to me—wasn't it obvious? *Hell of a lot better looking*—he was always saying what a good-looking people the Vietnamese were, how beautiful the women. But there must have been one in particular—one he could not forget. He had fallen in love over there—that was what all this passionate yearning was really about. Like Thomas Fowler, he had had a mistress, a mistress like Phuong.

He denied it. In fact he was—or pretended to be—vastly amused by my logic. There had been no Phuong, he assured me, laughing. Things didn't happen in real life the way they happened in novels. But I never believed him. She existed. And nothing easier for me than to imagine her, dressed in her sexy *ao dai*. Or undressed, her long black hair spread out on the pillow. I could see her fine hands with their slender wrists and polished oval nails as she prepared his opium pipes. Very young—younger even than I—and a thousand times lovelier . . .

The only Vietnamese person I had ever met happened also to be a young woman, her name rhymed with Phuong, and she was my aunt. My mother's brother, an army sergeant, had brought her and their infant son to America five years before, and for a time we all lived together in our apartment in the project, my parents and my two sisters and me, my uncle and his wife, who was pregnant again, and their son. My uncle had learned to speak Vietnamese, but my aunt's English was not yet good enough for us to get to know her well. In fact, I would never know her well. Coming home from school, I would find her watching television, a pair of chopsticks in one hand, a jar of hot chili peppers in the other. When I tasted just a shred of what she offered me, a blister rose immediately on my tongue. I did not dare to swallow. She laughed. "For you like eat napalm, right?" Right. And as she gazed in wonder at American soap operas, so I at her—until every last pepper in that jar was gone. Even pregnant she could squat with both feet flat on the edge of the bathtub and without losing her balance lean all the way over to wash her never-cut hair. When she was pleased with her little boy, she held up her thumb: "You number-one son!" She gave me manicures. Not much talk but plenty of giggles: two teenage girls. She gave me an *ao dai* that she had brought from home— tight turquoise tunic, loose white pants. We were about the same size then, but I never wore it—where would I have worn it? I wish I knew what had become of it, though.

Now I don't know whether to believe my own story about the journalist and the Vietnamese love of his life.

There were tears when I heard about his death, but they were at least partly tears of frustration (the exquisite suffering I had seen coming in fact never came)—I did not understand why I could not feel more. But at that age even a year is forever— almost nothing in my life was the same as it had been when we'd met—and I no longer thought much about him, about us.

One of my roommates was fully engaged in the women's lib- eration movement, in full surge at the time. I had left my copy of Graham Greene's book lying around, and she picked it up and read it and pronounced it *stomach turning.* She meant Phuong, of course: Fowler's Vietnamese girl, his twittering bird. Passive, childlike, undemanding, rarely speaking, always serving, inter- ested only in fashion, gossip about royalty, getting a husband, pleasing her man. "The quintessential male fantasy: the one-man whore." Everything my roommate was fighting against. "And you—you ought to be fighting, too, instead of lying around mop- ing about your Sexy Older Married Man." She had never met him, but she truly hated him. "Haven't heard from him, have you? Well, are you surprised? You weren't a human being, sister, you were just another tasty little morsel on that pig's plate." The only part of the book she liked was the part where Fowler goes to bed with a prostitute and can't get it up.

I still have that old paperback, much worn, dented on the spine from when my roommate threw it across the room. I take it down from the shelf. A short book, easy to get through on the long train ride back to Massachusetts. A good read—a detective story, a story of love and war. Here again Phuong twitters, Fowler wrestles with the temptation to be killed, and Alden Pyle, the most famous American in British literature, is killed—none of them very convincingly, at least not to me, not this time around. I can recall reading the book for the first time and being swept away, turning the last page with a sigh, wholly satisfied. Now Phuong, Pyle, even Fowler the narrator and main protagonist—none of them quite comes to life. They are like people one has heard about rather than people one knows, and with the best novels the reader always feels as though he or she had known the characters, and known them thoroughly, in real life. It's the American war that gives the book an amplitude, a resonance, and complexities it would not otherwise have. It's the American war—still in the future when the book was written—that made it a classic, to this day considered one of the most important novels written about Vietnam. Rereading it on the train, I can't help wondering what Rouenna would have made of it. I wonder what my aunt—a grandmother now, and yet another one who eventually ended up in New Jersey—would make of it.

And rereading brings this discovery: details I had for years remembered as being from the stories told by the journalist turn out actually to have come from Greene's book.

Graham Greene, British reporter in Vietnam, anti-American, estranged from his wife, afflicted with melancholy, smoker of opium . . .

"Up the street came the lovely flat figures—the white silk trousers, the long tight jackets in pink and mauve patterns slit up the thigh." So Fowler, looking out from the bar of the Hotel Continental. The street is the rue Catinat, after the defeat of the French changed to Tu Do ("Freedom")—the same street where the GI snapped the tiny bones of the pickpocket—after the defeat of the Americans changed to Dong Khoi ("Revolution"). Always, under whatever name, a hubbub of a street, filled with bars, hotels, cafés, restaurants, shops, and foreigners.

I never told Rouenna about the journalist, but I would think of him sometimes when we talked. Although their experiences of Vietnam were entirely different—so different it might as well have been two separate countries—at times I caught echoes. "Vietnam was the biggest thing that ever happened to me." Both of them said these exact words to me. Both of them described how happy they had been in Vietnam, and how for all the horrors and dangers of the war, no sooner had they left than they wanted only to go back again.

"I watched them with the nostalgia I knew I would feel when I had left these regions forever," Fowler goes on. And later in the book he utters his famous dreamy prediction "that in five hundred years there may be no New York or London, but they'll be growing paddy in these fields, they'll be carrying their produce to market on long poles wearing their pointed hats."

Long after the journalist had left New York for London, after whatever feelings I'd had for him had died and he had died and was all but forgotten, the sight of one of those pointed hats could fill me with romance.

A large envelope has come in the mail while I was away. My heart turns over when I see that it is from Rouenna's mother. In response to my request for a photograph, she has sent several, snapshots mostly, some black and white, some color. Only one of the photos is recent: Rouenna as memory might conjure her, only with longer, somewhat fuller hair. She is wearing a sweatshirt I have seen her wear before, and although she is sitting down, the way she fills the photo frame brings back the way she filled the doorway of her apartment the first time I saw her. Big smile. All of the other photos were taken at some time or other many years ago, and were it not for the eyes I'm not sure that I would recognize Rouenna. In the earliest photo she is holding a baby, the younger of her two brothers, I presume. The baby—enormous in those little-girl arms—is in a white bunting, and because his eyes have come out bright Polaroid-red, it looks (horribly, hilariously) as if Rouenna is holding a large white rabbit with a human snout. In the background can be seen the lower tinsel-fringed branches of a Christmas tree and—my heart turns over again—a portion of the identical linoleum tiles that covered the floors of all the housing project apartments. There are a few school portraits, a First Communion portrait, a blurry shot of a girl with angel's wings and drunken halo. All in pink for Senior Day—for a moment I think Rouenna is wearing a turban, but no, that is her own teased hair. Bubble cut, bubble skirt, fake pearls, short white gloves. Her nurse's uniform *fits* like a short white glove. ("What could have been worse? For a job that's so damn dirty and so physical, a straight white dress, white nylons, white shoes.

Naturally back then every nice girl had to wear a girdle no matter how firm. Nurses were told that girdles were good because they gave support to the back, in which case every surgeon should have been wearing one. But for me it felt like being constipated all the time. And even with the girdle, I can't tell you how many times I split a seam, turning a patient or stripping a bed. Thank god in Nam I got to work in fatigues. I wore a girdle under my uniform for the flight over, but that was the last time. In fact, liberation from that undergarment is one of the things I associate with Vietnam.")

Two photographs from army days. In one she is wearing her dress uniform, smile exaggerated to the point of mockery, thumb directing attention to her second lieutenant's "butter bar." Still stateside then. She would not be promoted to first lieutenant until she got to Vietnam. ("Rank—it didn't mean much, promotions came cheap during the war. I remember seeing this written on a wall at the Saigon airport: *If war is hell then rank be damned.* All the army nurses were officers, but that didn't mean shit to the men. You were still just a chick, not someone they were about to take orders from. And there were some who had a real nasty attitude about women in the service, they had some idea that we were all working on the side as whores. Like you really had to join the army, go halfway around the world, and work triple shifts up to your neck in shit while being rocketed—I tell you, some of these boys were dumb. These were the same kind of dumb kids who were fixed on the notion that in every whorehouse Victoria Charlies were lying in wait with razor blades up their vaginas. I got so sick of hearing that story—like there weren't enough real ways to lose your dick in Vietnam. Thank god all the men weren't like that. But the ones who believed those stories, those were the ones you had to watch out for. Just might give you what they thought you were looking for. It wasn't as bad for us as it was for the other women, the ones who weren't in the military but who went over with the USO, or the Red Cross volunteers, the doughnut dollies. Those girls were just dragged through the mud. It turns out a lot of people could not believe that any woman would want to go to Vietnam except for one reason.") And it wasn't only men who were hostile. Rouenna had bitter words for the stewardesses on the flight overseas. "There I was, only female on a plane with two hundred men. You'd think I'd stick out, but no, not to those bitches. To them I was invisible."

Some of the army doctors were against having any women in the war zone. "They wanted to keep it all male nurses. I remember there was this one doctor who felt real strongly about this, and he kept taking it out on me. There I am, picking maggots out of a hole that used to be this little guy's butt, and this doctor is carrying on about how we women don't belong there—as if we women hadn't been told by those lying recruiters that there was no way any nurse would end up in Vietnam unless she volunteered. I kept my cool, but inside I was seething and squirming like that wound I was trying to clean. The doctor had a can of Coke he was sipping from and at one point he had to break off and turn his attention to the next bed, and it occurred to me how I ought to slip one or two of those maggots in. Don't give me that look. This was a real bastard I'm talking about. A bad doctor, not up to his job. We called him Doctor Do Little. So quick to give up on a guy—guys who were real messed up but still might have had a tiny chance. The nurses and the corpsmen—we all hated him. In fact, there were two of them on that ward like that, one worse than the other, and that's what we called them: Doctor Do Little and Doctor Do Less.

"But Doctor Do Little was an exception. Most of the doctors were only too happy to have some round-eyes available. Though a lot of them had wives back home, those doctors, like doctors I've known everywhere, liked to sleep around. They were as generous with the Pill as they were with the Dexedrine—it was like jelly beans on Easter, just hold out your hand—and when one of the nurses got pregnant everyone knew it was on purpose, and why. It was your female equivalent of shooting yourself in the hand or foot, something you saw happening more and more as the war went on. I had already seen one or two cases while I was still stateside in training—cases where men had done damage to themselves, sometimes pretty severe. There was this one kid who asked to have a friend drive a jeep over him. Crushed both legs— he was a double amp! No different from the vets in the other beds! I said, Hell, soldier, you might as well have gone over and fought, spared your buddy the guilt and yourself the shame. Like I say, some of these guys? *Dumb.* And by the time I left Nam, the wards were filling up with self-wounded and malingerers of all kinds, men who would do just about anything to stay out of the field. The ones faking insanity were the worst. They'd all seen the same episode of *I Love Lucy*—you know: *Where am I? Who am I?* You just didn't know where to look. In the beginning I had a bad feeling about such men, I had no use for their kind, much less for draft dodgers—don't get me started on draft dodgers!— but I changed. I will be honest, there were times when I thought about getting pregnant or faking insanity myself. We all did."

In the other photograph Rouenna is wearing her much-loved fatigues, a helmet, and a flak jacket, as if she were on her way to her bunker, but she is grinning, she is flourishing a bottle of Johnnie Walker Red, and across the top of the picture is written *Hooch in my hooch!* She was fond of recalling the parties she had been to, the beer parties and the pot parties and the homesick-making barbecues. ("Did I tell you about the time some marines dragged a buffalo back to base and tried to cook it on a spit?" Tears of mirth rolled down her cheeks whenever she remembered this.) "When you're at a party and you're one of maybe two, three girls and the place is packed with men, it's easy to believe you are beautiful. That was another nice thing about Vietnam." The only time in her life when she thought she was beautiful. "Of course there was the issue of fraternization, but most of the nurses, if they wanted to date an enlisted man, they just went ahead. Sometimes they caught flak—from some lifer, say. But in general you could get away with a lot over there. There was an attitude, some of the women were just as infected with it as the men: What could they do to you? You were already *in* Vietnam."

Another nice thing: "You could eat like a pig and never gain weight because of all those long hours working on your feet, plus all the speed we took during a push." A steady diet of barbecued steak, Scotch, and reconstituted ice cream.

Food. "We used to sit around during mess sometimes and talk about foods we missed. Everyone would say what was the first food they were going to chow down just as soon as they got back to the world. A lot of people said a Big Mac. Others wanted lasagna, or fresh corn on the cob, or a big plate of some favorite thing their mother or girlfriend used to make. Me, it was always a tomato. A great big fat red Jersey tomato, like the kind we used to get from the farm stand. A nice fresh tomato with a whole crust of salt. I would think about it so much, I could feel the juice dripping down my chin. Would have traded a hundred thick steaks just for one."

Because it was in her mother's possession, I imagine this particular photo as having been mailed from overseas, enclosed with a letter, say—though I remember Rouenna telling me that she did not write many letters that year. Though not the oldest of the photographs, it is the most worn, dog-eared and creased as if it had been much handled. Or maybe this was how it had come in the mail (if it came in the mail): battered. But if I had been Rouenna, I would not have wanted to give this photograph away. I would have wanted to hold on to it. I would have taken good care of it, would have at least thought about having it enlarged and framed. Though at quick glance you might easily mistake her for a GI, I doubt whether Rouenna ever looked better. Or maybe that was the last thing she wanted: to be reminded how much better she looked then. How thin. Face so thin the eyes stand out. Big blue eyes. Big smile—always one to smile for the camera, it seems Rouenna was.

Hooch in my hooch. "I was always up for a party."

She said, "Even in a war you can find ways to have fun."

When I have looked at all the photographs and looked at them again, when I have spent a whole hour dreaming over them in spite of rumblings in my stomach, I go to make myself something to eat. While the soup is heating, I try to work out what it is that is bothering me. *A life in pictures*—the phrase sings in my head like a taunt. Go into any house, go to the place where the albums are kept, and you'll find pictures just like these— photographs taken on holidays and to commemorate special events—the family without such a collection would be strange. More often than not the photos are of poor quality, out of focus, over- or underexposed, weird lights and shadows and rabbit-eyes everywhere. Usually the person who took the picture was standing either too close or too far away. In fact, the badness of family photographs is one of the most familiar things about them, what makes them all seem so alike.

Ladling soup into a bowl, I glance up, see the way the photos lie, how I have laid them out, in rows, upon the table—like tarot cards. Only in this case it is not a future waiting to be read but a past. And sitting down at the table with my bowl and spoon, I slump a little with despair—it is as if a spell has been broken, and the futility of my project is laid bare.

Roro. A tall sinewy girl with a thatch of dirty-blond hair. So have I described her, but she is not here, she is not among the photos on the table. The naked pink-skinned creature that runs shrieking round and round my head—

Cunt!

I taste the soup without thinking, before it has had a chance to cool, and scald my mouth. I push the bowl away, swallowing soup, swallowing pain. With both hands I push the photographs away, push them right off the table, onto the floor, and in the cleared space I cross my arms, I rest my head.

Think, think—where were we that day? My place, we were at my place—the first time she was ever there. ("Looks like you just moved in.") Snatch of music through the open window, car radio, outrageously loud, electric guitar squeal, unmistakable. Jimi Hendrix, once of the Army Airborne himself. I saw it catch in her like a fishhook. "Oh, how that song used to rock Danang." I got up, went to the kitchen, got her another beer, and asked her to begin at the beginning. Why was she in Vietnam? Newark, nursing school, recruiters all over the place giving their pitch: Join the U.S. Army Nurse Corps, and we'll cover tuition—and don't you worry about ending up in any war. I said, But how could they lie to you—how could they get away with that? You must have been so angry! *I* was angry, on her behalf. I was furious, my blood was throbbing, I could easily have burst into tears. She rolled her eyes. She could not resist. *How could they lie to you*—mimicking me, all mousy-voiced indignation. *How could the big bad army get away with that?* Only time she was ever mean to me. Long swig of beer. Relax, kid, you got it wrong. They lied, all right, but that didn't affect me. I volunteered.

When I lift my head again, it is swimming. I stare dully ahead at the wall. A blank white wall—like all the walls in that apartment—crying out I suppose to most eyes for something: a painting, a poster, a mirror, a clock.

But stare at any blank space long enough, intently enough, and some image is sure to emerge.

A woman, clutching her head between her hands, her mouth wide open, screaming.

A fat, drunk, middle-aged woman, rocking and tapping her thigh to a thirty-year-old Jimi Hendrix song.

A foxy young army lieutenant, big blue eyes lit with pleasure and greed, biting into a giant tomato. Red juice and seeds drip down her chin.

Part TWO

My mother has sleeping sickness, Roro told the class.

The audiovisual presentation that week had been about disease in Africa. The boys had laughed and the girls had screamed at the sight of half-naked Africans with the ballooning limbs of elephantiasis, the stumps of leprosy, and uncontrollable shakes. These last victims, all skin and bone, were the ones with the sleeping sickness they had caught from flies.

Mrs. Stritch, no fan of Roro's, spoke to the ceiling through her teeth. I want everyone here to ignore what Miss Zycinski just said. Because it's a lie. And she knows it.

Of course she did. She had been making a *joke.* Never mind. Next time she would hold up a sign.

Every morning before leaving for school, Roro would make her mother a cup of instant coffee, mixing the granules as she'd been taught not with water but with milk. It was tricky, catching the milk in the little saucepan before it frothed up all over the stove—if she so much as yawned she might miss it, it happened that fast. Then what a mess. By the time she cleaned up, she'd be late for school. She stirred three sugar cubes into the coffee and popped four into her mouth to suck while waiting for the bus. Breakfast.

Home from school, she often found her mother still in bed, often asleep. The icky coffee cup sat on the floor. A roach sat in the cup. She knew her mother didn't have sleeping sickness or any other sickness, no matter what she said, and that her father was right on the button when he called her a lazy this and a lazy that. After all, it wasn't as if she were dying like the Africans. And just because she spent the day in bed didn't mean she slept the whole time. She wheeled the TV set in from the living room and watched it for hours, cartoons in the morning, soaps in the afternoon, and though she wasn't getting fat (she smoked too much), she wasn't wasting away like the Africans, either. *Said* she was sick—too sick to cook and no appetite—but the area around the bed was littered with crumpled cellophane wrappers. Roach picnic. Her favorite thing was mixing salty with sweet, a bag of pretzels or chips with a couple of Hershey bars. Said she was too weak even to pick up those wrappers or carry that dirty cup to the sink—but there was strength enough in the hand that shot out when Roro rebelled. ("It's your mess, why don't *you* clean it up?")

Roro would have gladly let Sleeping Beauty lie, except that she knew there'd be hell to pay. Nothing riled her father worse than to come home from work and find her mother still in bed. It had happened once too often, and that time he had dragged her out of the bed by the hair. Her mother, who had been fast asleep when he grabbed her, had been so scared she wet the floor. And then he did a terrible thing. He pushed her face in it, he wiped the puddle on the floor with her hair.

If Roro ever breathed a word about what happened that day, her mother promised to skin her alive. It was all Roro's fault anyway, for not waking her. *Smack!* After that, both mother and daughter were more careful. There was just enough time between Roro's and her father's coming home to get the room picked up, the bed made, the TV back in its place, and something started for supper. The last was not so important. Her father welcomed any excuse to order out. Food delivered to your door—a novelty then—how could you not love it? Three choices: pizza, chicken, or chinks. Whichever they chose, it was wonderful how the dreary little kitchen bloomed into life around the steaming cartons.

The boys were gone. Grandma Marie, her father's mother, who lived nearby and visited often, saw how it was. A ten-year-old doing most of the housework and child care. I'm taking the boys to live with me until you two come to your senses, she told their parents, and don't try to stop me. No one dreamed of trying to stop her. But Roro could have screamed. *What about me?* Bitter tears. But soon her heart lifted. Life was so much easier now. Scraping burnt milk off the stove and picking up candy wrappers was nothing compared to changing diapers. Before, her work was never done—she was Cinderella, only with two bratty little brothers instead of two big mean stepsisters.

She could have had it worse. Look around: the project was full of Cinderellas. Girls who could not come out to play until they'd finished scrubbing the bathroom, girls who were kept home from school to help their mothers, mothers who would have kept them out of school altogether if there hadn't been a law. Girls like the Deane sisters, from families that brought forth a child every year, who instead of having to make do with dolls arrived at the playground wheeling the real red-faced, squalling, stinky thing. Many years later, the officers' club at Long Binh, loudmouthed lieutenant colonel holding forth: *I want to know what kind of people—little kids breaking their backs in the fields—no child labor laws—a crying shame*—and they all came swarming back: the little maids and mothers of the projects. Little beauticians: girls who had to do their mothers' nails and roll their hair and squeeze their blackheads—oh god, what if her mother made her do that! What if her father made her do what Mr. John made his daughter do: wash his feet every day when he came home from work.

The Johns lived two floors down. Mr. John was a large, quiet man who worked as a security guard in a bank (on his feet all day). Sissy John, who was also large for her age, and quiet, never complained about her nightly duty, though she seemed ashamed, as if she knew her father went too far. For his footbath he would strip down to his shorts. Roro had witnessed the ritual once, by accident. Most whites living in the project did not want their children playing with black children, and Roro's parents had their own rule: All right for Roro to play with Sissy outdoors, but they didn't want her going into Sissy's apartment or inviting her into theirs—that was getting too close. One day when it was raining sheets, Roro's mother ran out of cigarettes. She gave Roro two dimes and told her to go down and try to buy some from Sissy's mother, a Kool addict like herself. When Mrs. John opened the door, Roro could see right into the kitchen where

Mr. John sat wearing nothing but a pair of light-blue shorts. Sissy, who never once looked up, was kneeling on the floor soaping one long, pink-soled foot with her bare hands in a plastic tub full of sudsy water. Mr. John had his eyes almost closed, he had a little smile on his face, he was curling and uncurling his toes, he was in heaven. He did not mind at all being seen in his shorts, it was as if Roro weren't even there—like Sissy, he ignored her completely. But then that was his way. Mr. John was one of the few fathers Roro was not afraid of. He moved so slowly and seemed always off somewhere in a world of his own. The half-closed eyes, the dreamy little smile—as though he were remembering something pleasant—were habitual, and he did not beat his children. In a world where the beating of children was taken for granted, this was something. The norm was men coming home after eight hours or more of taking orders at low-paying jobs, fingers already fiddling with belt buckles as they walked in the door, demanding to know which one of their goddamn kids had screwed up that day.

Mrs. John, dragging on a precious Kool right then, looked at the dimes in Roro's palm and shook her head. Tell your mama I can't be selling no cigarettes to no little girl. She should come down and ask me herself.

Upstairs, Roro's mother flew into a rage. She just wants me to beg her, that's all. She just wants to make a white woman come crawling and beg her. Well, she can go to hell.

Other times Roro heard her mother say, I don't like the way that black bitch looks at me. Like I don't know what she's thinking. She's thinking *white trash*. That's what she's saying to herself. Just let her come up and say it to my face.

How her mother could be so sure what Mrs. John was saying to herself, Roro did not understand. But looking back one day, she would think her mother was probably right.

And maybe she really was a little sick, her mother. No denying at times she was in pain. You don't cry like that—sobs so convulsed they bring up vomit—unless there's real pain. A look that sometimes came over her face, as if someone had just shown her a picture of herself in old age or dying. That sad, that scared. Or that other look, not sad or scared but just plain miserable, as if the end could not come soon enough. She didn't have sleeping sickness, but she was tired all right. And if she wasn't dying, some part of her, maybe even the best part, was withering away.

Hard times to live through, they would be hard to look back on as well. As a grown woman, Roro would avoid dwelling on her childhood. When the memories came anyway, when—just as she was trying to fall asleep, say—they came rushing at her, god knows why from god knows where, and would not be chased away, she was surprised at the mixture of feelings they brought, the tenderness and the shame.

Her father could not hold a job. He had a temper and without fail would get into some dispute with the boss. He was just that sort of man who cannot take orders, who cannot stand to have some other man (or god forbid some woman) tell him what to do. Roro did not understand how he had ever made it through the army. But her mother, who had known him since high school, said he hadn't always been that way, and Grandma Marie said he wouldn't be that way now if he would lay off the bottle. But father and mother both liked to drink, and often when they'd been drinking they were at their best, lots of laughs and all lovey-dovey. Both could sing, and sometimes when they were drinking (and only when they were drinking) they would start singing together, and those were the times when Roro loved her parents with all her heart. They had real talent, they could harmonize, they sang hit songs you heard on the radio, and they sounded just as good—Roro didn't understand why they didn't shape up and get themselves onto a stage somewhere, they were as good as anyone you saw on *Ed Sullivan.* And they had the looks, too. Her mother had that fine coloring that Roro would see again on a number of young Polish women when she moved to Williamsburg: pale skin, smoky eyes, and hair that was naturally the same reddish-brown shade that so many other women tried to get from henna. (Her mother herself later did a stupid thing, first bleaching her hair blond, then dyeing it black, then blond again, then black—blond—black—and when she wanted to go back to natural, either out of spite or because it had really forgotten her hair would not grow in that old beautiful color, and she too had to resort to henna.)

Her father's hair was so blond you might have thought *he* used bleach, and his eyes were a hard bright blue. See him at the helm of one of those Viking ships. He was tall and long-limbed, with a head like a chiseled boulder. Once, when the drinking and the laughing and the harmonizing got to be too much, someone in the building called the police. The two cops who arrived might have been father and son. The younger one was unable to take his eyes off Roro's mother, who seemed to have forgotten that she was only half-dressed, nothing over her leopard-skin push-up bra. The other had eyes only for Roro's father, who was lurching about the room on stilted legs, arms extended for balance, like Frankenstein's monster. Stiff as a rod himself, the cop kept saying, Easy now, big fella. Easy, easy.

Her father was *too* big. In their cluttered house, he was for-ever knocking into things. Though you'd think the furniture had knocked into *him,* the way he kicked it back. Never knew when *he* was going to boil over, like the milk. His stomach growling was like thunder, his sneeze rattled the windowpanes. He was prone to hay fever and to headaches: tension. He was always tense. An animal turning in circles in a tight space, growing wilder and wilder, don't get too close. A dog or a horse that needed to break out and run run run.

Hard-muscled though he was, he liked soft women, fleshy women, women like his wife about whom you could say as people said then *fat in all the right places.* He had no use for skinny women, whom he mocked one and all as "Olyve Oyl." But after the third baby, Roro's mother began to plump up, and her husband didn't like that, either. Threatened to chain her to the bed and throw her scraps. The way he said it—well, he wasn't smiling when he said it. She got that weight off fast. But not so many years later, when her mother started putting on pounds like no tomorrow, Roro saw that her father not only did not make good his threat, not only did not seem to care, but did not seem even to notice. Of course by that time he himself had blown up, all his thick muscle turned to thicker flab.

But it was nonsense to talk about laying off the bottle. Drink might be the source of trouble, but it was also just the thing to make trouble go away. His Scotch and sodas, her rum and Cokes—where would her parents have been without them? Didn't everyone need sometimes to laugh and sing? What ani-mal, for that matter, would have taken away her mother's Kools? Wasn't it obvious how they comforted her—how she reached for them at the first sign of stress? No, as far as Roro was concerned, these things were godsends, like the TV. They helped make life bearable, and she did not want to think how it would have been without them. Never forget that week the set was on the blink and all they had to look at was one another. So please, no more talk about laying off the bottle.

And sometimes, when her mother was all dressed up and made up to go out, Roro would behold her and know perfectly why the woman had such a hard time with dirty dishes and diapers. See that face on the cover of a magazine. When the Avon lady came calling she said, You are just the kind of beautiful girl we like to think of using our products, and Roro forgave her mother everything.

Several men who lived in the project worked in a large bakery across the kill in New Jersey. For a while Roro's father was one of them. The men had a car pool. Some days they would gather after work in one or another of their apartments for a beer. Roro, in her room struggling with her homework, was drawn out by her mother's horrified squeals. Around the kitchen table the men were doubled over with laughter, they had let it slip how they would spit into the custard and jelly that went into the doughnuts made in the bakery. And that is why for the rest of her life, Roro would not be able to eat doughnuts. And there came a day when she'd reached her teens when she lost her appetite completely—the only time in her life this ever happened to her, and it did not last long—and during that time the memory of those men haunted her. She would remember the story, she would see them laughing and hawking around the kitchen table and imagine that everywhere food was prepared there lurked some such man fouling every mouthful. (And in the army, sharing a pizza with a couple of recruits: one piece left—who gets it? *Ah do!* cried the redneck, hurling a gob at the slice.)

Roro's mother had the nasty habit at times of using her saliva to clean Roro's face, and when she did Roro would squirm like a torture victim. Then a car hit Vicky Merz. Roro did not actually see the car hit Vicky, she arrived a few minutes later, on her way home from the store, and saw her sprawled in the road, and the blood on the back of her wheat-blond head looked just like jelly oozing from a doughnut.

Not a bad accident, luckily, and Vicky survived to become the most important person in fifth grade.

Accidents happened, and children especially were prone to them—everyone knew that.

How did the Robinsons' baby lose three fingers?

Door accidentally slammed on his hand.

What happened to Kimberly's eye?

Fork slipped.

The day an unearthly shriek rent the air: someone's canary had flown into a hot oven.

The strangest accident of all befell a deaf-mute girl who was called Happy. So strange, people described it not just as an accident this time but as a *freak* accident. For some reason Happy was down in the basement, where she got a notion to straddle a large metal trash basket, and somehow a prong of this trash basket managed to work its way loose and pierced her privates. She's in the hospital now, her mother said. And what had happened to her mother's face? Had a tooth out. And she smiled, delicately, and there indeed were missing not one but one and a half teeth.

Accidents happened, and it was not true what was said, that God protected small children and drunks. Like Humpty Dumpty, Mr. Deane, bricklayer, drunk, had a great fall from a wall. He would not be home for a very long time, and he would not walk ever again.

Bad things happened, understood, and it was not true that lightning never struck twice. Mr. Deane was still in the hospital when he suffered another accident, this one freak. When the aide who had taken him out for some air turned the wheelchair around, they saw a trail of blood. One of Mr. Deane's paralyzed feet had got caught under the chair. By the time they saw the blood, the foot had been scraped to the bone.

The Deanes were too many for their apartment and were on the waiting list for something larger. Meanwhile they had to sleep five or six to a room. Mrs. Deane had some problem with her eyes and sometimes wore dark, greenish-black glasses that made her look like a blind person. She had no telephone, and once when she came to use the Zycinskis', after she left, Roro's mother swabbed alcohol over the receiver and every surface Mrs. Deane had touched. A tooth for every baby, people used to say—and poor Mrs. Deane had a smile like Halloween, a few crooked tombstones and some nubs that were the same greenish-black color as her glasses. Of her fourteen children, only three were boys. One was a crib death, another was killed at the battle of Hue, and the third, who also fought in Vietnam, came home safe but later died of AIDS. Sometimes lightning strikes and strikes.

The job at the bakery lasted less than a year. Doughnut maker, supermarket cashier, plumber's assistant, carpenter's assistant, school bus driver, taxi driver, furniture mover, groundskeeper, window washer, car washer, dishwasher—Roro's father kept none of these jobs very long. And what difference did it make? *A job was a job* and one was just like another, and none was worth hanging on to *for Chrissake* when it was gone it was gone and *so long as you weren't afraid to get your hands dirty* there'd always be some kind of work for you. *And no matter what* he was never out of work for more than a few weeks at a time, his wife had never had to take a job, and he had never *stooped to welfare.* He was very proud of that, not stooping to welfare. But the truth was, if it hadn't been for those hardworking, hoarding immigrant grandparents, the Zycinskis would never have made it through those years. And it was the grandparents' dying off that would bring about a steady improvement in the family's life, enabling them first to move out of the project to a duplex, and eventually to buy a one-family house of their own.

The duplex was not really much of an improvement. The main thing it had going for it was that it was not the project. Not that it was far from the project, either. At least all the new neighbors were white. The Zycinskis didn't own the duplex, of course. Still: it was one giant step closer to a real home.

The boys were back. They were growing up, they were quite a devilish handful now, Grandma Marie with her ailing heart could not keep up with them. What a blessing, then, to have more space, not to mention a porch and half of a small backyard. And now the Zycinskis could also have what they had always wanted but in the project were forbidden to have.

The dog was still a puppy when satisfaction with the new place began to fade, at least for Roro's mother, who would grow to hate it. They were too close to the water, for one thing: it was always damp. And where there is water there must be rats, and she had always been terrified of all rodents, even harmless squirrels. Though no rat had yet been seen indoors, a particularly huge one appeared one day, dragging its belly along the back porch. Roro's mother later dreamed of that rat and its hundreds and hundreds of hairless pink babies squeezing through the keyhole, and though it was only a dream, in the state she was working herself into the line between dream and reality was blurring.

They were near the water, they were near the sea, and where there is sea there must be gulls, and Roro's mother was haunted by their high, aching, eerie cries, as mournful to her ears as foghorns—another sound you could not escape being near the water. She hated gulls as she hated crows—both were associated in her mind with Death. (She would take the Hitchcock movie when she saw it completely to heart, she would have no trouble at all believing that birds, to say nothing of rats, were capable of conspiring to kill people.) And then came this blow: the nice young childless couple who lived in the eastern half of the duplex and with whom the Zycinskis had made friends moved out, and in moved a bunch of beatniks—beards, berets, bongos, and all. No ordinary nuclear family but five adults and seven children, who related to whom unclear. Roro's mother hated the records they played (jazz) but was afraid to complain because of other sounds she sometimes heard coming from there, chanting or droning, the same word repeated endlessly, it sounded like, some word with an *r* and a *d*. *Red red red red red?* Though the electricity was working fine, they often used candles to light the house, and the pungent smell of frankincense seeped through the walls, the smell of mass—a black mass, what else, they were practicing some kind of witchcraft over there, and she could not let go of the fear that Something Evil was headed toward them.

Dread dread dread dread dread? If the rats and birds didn't get her, the beatniks would.

And now it happened that Roro came down with sleeping sickness—like one long wicked flu that would not go away. Aches and fevers, swollen glands. She missed so much school, she would have to be left back. This would upset her no end later, but right now she was too sick to care. All she wanted was to sleep. But no matter how much sleep she got, she was never rested.

Mononucleosis. Roro was not the only one in her junior high school to get it. There were a lot of rumors. You got it from kissing, you got it from being Jewish, you got it from kissing someone Jewish—all kinds of things were said. It wasn't a real disease at all, you got it because you were mental. (Rumors: when the time came to join the army, Rouenna, filling out medical forms, vaguely remembered hearing something about the military not taking you if you'd had mono, and so lied.)

A strange disease, with a strange name, which no one seemed to know much about, certainly not how to cure it. How contagious was it? None could say, but the doctor thought it couldn't hurt to send the boys away, so off they went, to Grandma Eva, in Brooklyn, this time. (Marie had died.)

Though the doctor explained that Roro's mother had never had mononucleosis and that she could not possibly have given it to their daughter, Roro's father insisted that this must be what had happened, and that was what he told everyone. He wanted sympathy, he felt immensely sorry for himself, it was like living with a pair of zombies, he griped. Now, he himself had just the opposite trouble: he was a great ball of restless energy, he had no desire to sleep, he was getting by on two, three hours a night. His headaches grew fiercer, worse than they had ever been, he was living on codeine, but he was still able to work. It was mostly manual labor these days. Construction of the bridge over the Narrows had begun, the great Staten Island building boom was getting under way, and there was always some contractor somewhere needing extra hands and willing to flout union or government regulations.

But not even long days of physical exertion could knock him out. Late into the night he would sit up alone among the delivery cartons that were piling up on every surface in the filthy kitchen. Pizza, chicken, or chinks. From time to time Roro would wake from one of her feverish dreams to the equally nightmarish spectacle of her father carrying drunkenly on, talking and singing to himself, bringing his fist like a sledgehammer down on the table (a game: see if he could get a roach to flip over on its back before he smashed it). The dog, King, a scrawny, swaybacked German shepherd, now full grown and fully aware of its condition (its days were numbered), lay paralyzed under its master's feet.

But he wasn't always alone, her father. Waking and listening, Roro would think that it couldn't be just him out there making all that noise. He had some of his buddies over, some of the men he worked with, and he was telling them the story, his sob story, his crying-into-his-beer story: how his wife had kissed a Jew and got the sleeping sickness and given it to his daughter and driven his sons from the house to live with his mother-in-law now that his own poor dear sweet mother—oh!

Once, Roro could have sworn there was a woman with him, a woman with a nagging, sing-song voice. Not her mother. And to this woman also her father told the story. But it was never clear whether he really believed this story and that wife and daughter were suffering from the same illness, or whether he kept telling it just so he could keep telling his joke. *Stereonucleosis!* That's what we got in this here house! We got stereonucleosis!

He and the neighbors were at constant war. When the noise got to be too much, the beatniks, not having it in them to call The Man, tried again and again to reason with him. Mistake. Now, to drown out his singing—and the yelps of the dog when he stomped it—they turned their records way up loud. They pounded their bongos in response to his fists. They burned so much incense, you would have thought they were trying to fumigate the place of him. They chanted, they droned, and if Roro's mother was right they did something more. Something to plant the germs of what would become his own wasting disease, from which, in another five years' time and after much suffering, he'd be *dead dead dead dead dead.*

One day in the spring of 1980, cleaning out her mother's closets, Rouenna opened an old heart-shaped candy box and found a sheaf of letters. Ancient letters, the paper so dry it crumbled. The earliest scrawled in pencil on blue-lined paper torn (hastily, carelessly) from a high school notebook. Faded, but legible. *Math is so Boring but I am not listening, I am sitting here counting all the ways that I Love You.*

Love letters. From her father to her mother. Even a few poems (poetry! her father!), and these Rouenna could not bring herself to read. Reading the letters (but she only skimmed them) was excruciating enough.

You had to know that day we did it that first time that there could never be anyone else for ME, *that I would* DIE *to make you* HAPPY, *and I would* KILL *anyone who tried to keep us* APART *like your father did that time. You had to feel it* WAY DEEP INSIDE, *like I did that time, all that* BURNING LOVE.

Teenage lovers (BURNING, CRAZY, MISUNDERSTOOD), soon to be APART. Most of the letters in the Valentine box had been written while her father was in the army. The ones from overseas told almost nothing about what was happening right then in the war; they were all set in the future. When he came home (*and don't you worry, I* WILL *come home to you, Baby, just like I promised, soon as we get these japs beat, which I promise you* WILL NOT *be long*), they would settle down. They would have it all: marriage, children, a beautiful house with a beautiful garden (*because I know how Baby loves flowers*), a dog (*because I know how much you love them*), and any other thing her baby heart desired.

She was his Angel, his Most Beloved Girl. He sent her *Love until the end of time (and one day more).* He had a picture and a curl of hair that he kept in a pouch tied to his dog-tag chain *so you are always with me.* Now and then he took them out to show off to the other men *so they could feel jealous.* None of them could have a girl back home half as fine as his. No girl in the world had prettier colored hair.

One letter had been ripped into little pieces, then lovingly reassembled and taped back together.

Sitting on the floor of her mother's bedroom closet (her mother out at a matinee with her soon-to-be third husband), Rouenna was amazed. Had she read these letters before? Never. How was it, then, that she knew what they said?

Her *hand* remembered.

"'I been thinking a lot about how much I love you, baby, and how when I get home—' Hey, put 'love' all in capitals and underline it, okay?"

"Draw a heart around her name, 'cause that's what I always do."

"—shrapnel: s-h-r-a-p—"

The addressees were mostly women. Girlfriends and wives but also mothers. "Please kiss Daddy and Piglet and Gramps but save the biggest kiss of all Mama for you."

Instead of a letter, sometimes a poem. Once, a prayer for a newborn son. "May you never know this thing called war."

And the ones who wrote back, who sent letters and packages from home—these were mostly women, too. And as there were men who needed to have letters written, there were men who needed to have letters read.

"'Precious Son, I pray to God this letter finds you safe.'"

"Come on, Zycinski, do something useful. He's a gork, you know he can't hear you."

Some things she knew she would never forget. Some things would be always with her.

"'Darling, I don't know how to tell you this, but I will never be able to touch you again.'"

How she bent to the task, taking the words down on a page of USO stationery, and her pen started skidding all over the place. Oh, my god, she thought, how is he going to, what is he going to— How she started to laugh. How she could not stop. But she and that marine sergeant, they were pals, they had hit it off from the day he'd been brought in, and the first thing she'd asked once he was stabilized was where he was from, and he

gasped *Staten Island.* He was no kid, not his first tour, not his first
Purple Heart, either. He knew what was what, and he lay silent
now, waiting for her to pull it together, but she didn't, she
couldn't, until he lost control himself and started laughing, too.
That was it: the unforgettable, the image that would always be
with her: him lying there helplessly throwing up his stumps. How
she dropped the pen, and it went skittering under the bed, and
you would have thought that was the funniest thing that ever
happened: the two of them laughed even harder. Rouenna was
beside herself, she stamped her feet, she doubled up, the paper
and pad she'd been writing on sliding to the floor, and when she
sat back again she was looking straight at the head nurse—
where'd she come from? Bad-news face. Rouenna was sure she
was going to get blasted, but the head nurse just marched her to
the nurses' station, sat her down with a glass of water, and left her
alone to work it out.

Back in the world, you always knew how a story like that
would come out sounding: crazy, sick, unbelievable. How you
could never explain that it was the kind of thing that happened
every day.

But over there nobody would come down on you for a lapse
like that. Everyone understood. The thing that was not so easily
forgiven was letting all your feelings hang out. No one ever really
likes a sensitive plant, and the nurse who failed to hide how
much all the suffering and dying was getting to her did not win
friends. You broke down in private if you had to. And of course
at one point or another everyone had to. It happened all the time:
you'd open the door to a linen closet, say, or to the supply room,
and behold some nurse supposedly on smoke break, doubled up,
rocking, in one case literally writhing on the floor (for an instant

Rouenna thought *seizure*), biting her hand to keep from crying out. What did you do? Did you step up and put your understanding sisterly arms around her? Hell no. You got whatever you'd come for and beat it. Minutes later she'd be back on the job. No one said a word. Everyone knew how everyone was feeling all the time, no need for words. Words couldn't do justice, anyway. Everyone knew that.

And everyone knew the story about the nurse at Chu Lai who'd been raped in the middle of an attack. On her way to the hospital, jumped from behind. *Turn your head you're dead.* He had to raise his voice above the din. She never saw his face. He told her to count to a hundred after he left. She didn't count at all, just waited a bit, then crawled out of the trench and reported to triage. This was at the height of Tet. ("What was I supposed to do? Men lying dead, bleeding or in pieces all over the place— what was I supposed to do, raise a fuss?")

Another story that was not going to play well back home. But that was the kind of nurse they needed over there. No sensitive plants.

In Vietnam the ghost of her father—not as she remembered him but as a young GI—visited Rouenna often. She had grown up knowing that one of the reasons he never had much trouble finding work despite his bad job history had to do with his war record. Somewhere, maybe in this same closet where she had found his letters, were his medals. Somewhere was a brittle yellowed clipping from the *Staten Island Advance.*

All I want is to kill every slant eye I meet and go home.

It was one of many surprises waiting for Rouenna in Vietnam: her dead father's ghost appearing regularly among all those soldiers. Bigger surprise: he was a comfort to her.

Letters. Once, about a month after she arrived, Rouenna received a thick envelope from some kids she didn't even know, a troop of Girl Scouts from the same Jersey town where, in the early sixties, the Zycinskis had bought their first house. *Dear Lieutenant Zycinski.* She was their good deed for the day. The letters were all much the same, the wording almost identical, and full of mistakes. *We want you to no that you are thinking of you.* She read about half before throwing them away. Next alert, she entertained herself under her bed writing imaginary letters back to those little green berets, describing some of the things she had seen. One month in-country, and already she was feeling this way. (Many years later, at the time of the Gulf War, she would hear about groups soliciting contributions: *Your Twenty Dollars Can Buy a Lonely Soldier a Christmas Gift.* And she would remember those gift boxes arriving at the base, each holding a nickel bag of potato chips, an apple, and a large chocolate chip cookie. But the apple had rolled around a lot on its way overseas. One bruised apple, and some sweet and salty crumbs. *We want you to no that you are thinking of you.*)

Surprises, gifts. Her last stateside leave, just days before she was to fly to Saigon, a van pulled up to the house. From an Italian bakery: a red, white, and blue sheet cake. The baker was an immigrant whose son had been among the first American troops to fall in the war. She-who-never-cries cried then.

The cake went straight into her mother's deep freeze. Rouenna would not let anyone touch it.

It's not that I am afraid to die. It's the thought I may never see you again.

The new guys say the girls back home are wearing skirts that barely cover their behinds. You know I'd be ashamed if this was you.

I am the only one of my squad who survived the attack, my buddies all died on the hill.

I'm thinking one day maybe I will write a book telling the truth about this war. I figure I could dictate the whole thing like this letter.

Is it snowing on the rez?

There were times when a soldier made you promise that, if he didn't pull through, you would write a letter to his loved ones describing how he died, a duty that could almost make you wish you had died yourself. Many of those letters ended up being identical, too. "We gave him enough morphine so that he wasn't in pain. He couldn't speak but he looked peaceful." Some things you'd blow your own hand away before you'd write them down.

If she came across any of her own letters during this spring cleaning, Rouenna knew that she would not read them.

Nothing had prepared her. Nothing *could have* prepared her. Not the gunshot and stabbing victims she had seen while a student nurse at the hospital in Newark. Not the war wounded convalescing on the wards at Fort Ord, where she was stationed after her eight weeks of officers' basic training at Fort Sam Houston. It was not just that she had never seen bodies so mangled (*torn limb from limb* was not just an expression in Nam). It was that she lacked the experience to treat them.

"Now listen up, lieutenant. The next time you decide you don't know what the hell you're doing, try deciding it ten seconds sooner."

Once she had adjusted (a miracle, how you did adjust) to living and working (though never, like some, to sleeping) through rocket attacks, once she'd learned how to tell incoming from outgoing, she stopped worrying so much that she, too, might get

hurt in this war. Though nurses did get hurt and even killed in
Vietnam, it was not this that Rouenna prayed to be spared but
the worse eventuality that she herself would do harm—the
Young Nurse's Prayer. Most of the army nurses were in their
early twenties and not long out of school. Rouenna had eight
months' nursing experience when she arrived in-country: more
than some. You looked to the veterans, those well into their
tours, to senior nurses with five, ten years of nursing behind
them, but these women had their hands full. Doctors rarely
wasted time helping nurses, army, wartime, no exception. As for
the corpsmen, they took orders from *you.*

Mass casualties, massive wounds (and rare was the body
wounded in only one part): disaster was never more than one
move, one hesitation away.

"You learn on the job," the head nurse, a captain on her second tour, told her. Calm. As if Rouenna had just joined the typing
pool.

"Got to get your feet wet sometime," one surgeon liked to
say. Here, that meant wet with blood.

And if there was one thing that troubled your sleep, that
laced your first weeks with anxiety so intense you were sure
you'd die from *it* sooner than from any shell, it was the fear
that—not necessarily through your incompetence or anyone
else's but because such a thing simply could not be avoided in
hell—some living would go out with the dead.

Here was another story making the rounds: corpsman zip-
ping dead grunt into body bag, gets zipper up to grunt's chin,
grunt pops his eyes open: "Hey, man, what the fuck?"

That had been somewhere else, of course, on someone else's
watch, far away, down in the Delta, and that's probably all it was,

another story, the kind of story that got told during a war, probably every war, it even sounded like something you'd heard somewhere before. Unverified and of uncertain origin, like the story about the nurse raped at Chu Lai, or the rumor about Washington planning to drop the A-bomb, only they couldn't pull out all the troops first or Hanoi would get suspicious (and do what exactly was never quite clear), so they were just going to evacuate the top brass, who'd be airlifted out at the last minute. The whores with the razor blades between their legs, the snipers waiting to pick you off just as you were about to board your freedom bird home. Or, in a different key, the navy nurse who'd hanged herself when she learned that the anesthesiologist to whom she'd considered herself wed had a real wife back in the real world. Et cetera. And after all, the way the story about the grunt in the body bag was told, it was a *funny* story. But they all knew how it could happen, here in the belly of chaos, during a big push, say, with more than a hundred casualties arriving in a couple of hours, people working shifts up to two and three days straight without sleep, sometimes passing out right on top of a patient, the wonder would have been if it hadn't happened, somewhere, at least once, maybe even more often, though you sure as shit were not going to be the one to come right out and say *It happened.* Which was why, whenever the story got told ("Hey, what the fuck?"), the response, even from those who had heard it before, was hysterical laughter.

And not long after the story reaches Rouenna for the first time, the following takes place on the helipad outside the hospital where she is reporting for duty. Men running back and forth carrying wounded from helicopters to receiving ward. Set apart, a pile of dead. At the bottom of the pile, an arm—a hand catches her eye: it moves, the fingers wiggle. Rouenna shouts, attracting the attention of the nearest person, a doctor racing past with a gurney. "Dig him out!"

A few minutes later, as she is twisting a tourniquet, the doctor comes up and informs her through tight lips that she is seeing things. Rouenna is mortified.

That evening: happy hour at the officers' club, drinking her third Scotch and soda at the bar, smoking Kool after Kool. The hand won't stop waving.

Was she seeing things? How about this: the guy was alive, salvageable even, but in all the confusion got tossed out by mistake. Then the weight of all those other bodies thrown on top of his crushed the last bit of life left in him. And that was what she saw, the final spasm.

Suddenly a hand drops down spiderlike in front of her face. The doctor, sneaking up behind her. "Buy you a drink?"

"You son of a bitch."

He had rank on her, but he was laughing too hard not to let it go.

Later that night, one of the corpsmen came to find her. "With all due respect, ma'am, when we got to it? That arm wasn't even attached. Had to be your imagination." He'd brought some weed, help ease her mind. Then they fucked, rank be damned.

She got over it. You couldn't brood over this sort of thing and still do your job. She figured later that the corpsman had lied to her about the arm being detached, just to squelch all doubt. But she knew how your mind could play that kind of trick on you. Seeing things, hearing things, imagining that things had happened other than they really had—it was all part of the strain.

For a week after one of the helicopter pilots was shot down (still missing when the war came to an end), Rouenna would spin around on her heel with her arms thrown wide, certain she had just heard his unique, much imitated hee-*haw*, hee-*haw*. And in the heavy monsoon season, when it seemed as if God were trying to drown the war, you'd begin to hear things after a while, under the rain's tattoo. Voices, laughter, someone singing, applause, hisses, heavy breathing, horses whinnying, a band tuning, a telephone ringing, a heart beating—louder and louder like the heart in that story you had to read in high school. "When You Wish Upon a Star," the Hail Mary, the Pledge of Allegiance, the theme from *Lassie*, your name. Someone calling your name. (*Be right there, Mom.*) Hee-*haw*, hee-*haw*.

Or take the day Rouenna arrived at Tan Son Nhut Airport, after that sleepless twenty-four-hour flight, her dress uniform skirt now accordion-pleated, sweltering in her nylons and girdle, stepping for the first time into that heat, that blistering, mouth-of-the-dragon heat, the air fetid with something never smelled before (fish frying in kerosene?), mincing across the tarmac in high heels mercilessly pinching her flight-swollen feet, her very first teetering baby steps in the land of South Vietnam—

From the ground she saw nothing but combat boots. Then a green forest closing in. *A sick nurse. Just what we need around here.* She spent the next three days tossing on a sweat-soaked cot, feverish and nauseated, that dig coming back and back at her, each time a little sharper, and always followed by gales of male laughter. And even though she'd been told that this kind of thing happened, and she was hardly the first new guy to fall ill upon arriving in-country, Rouenna was ashamed. An ignominious beginning, something she felt she would have to live down. (Not to mention the spanking-clean fatigues and bright squeaky boots that every new guy was so self-conscious about.)

But by the time she was well, by the time she had in-processed at Long Binh and boarded the C-130 that would take her up-country to her first duty station, an evacuation hospital in Danang, she knew that those sharp words and the jeering laughter had never occurred. They too had been her imagination, her own fear and shame making themselves heard.

But the hand, the hand—

—had continued to haunt her the whole time she was there. Now it reached across ten years, and the bloodstained fingertips—cold as death all right—grazed her cheek. So that she had to get up from the floor of her mother's closet, go into the bathroom, and throw water on her face.

She came back into the bedroom on tiptoe, scarcely breathing, and lay down on her mother's bed. As gently as if the room were filled with infants she had just got to sleep. *Hush.* Usually at this hour the room was sunny, but it was partly cloudy today, and the light was dim. Except for her mother's pit bull, Gigi, asleep on a sofa downstairs, Rouenna was the only one home. This was not the same house the Zycinskis had bought when they moved to New Jersey from Staten Island. That house had been sold—a move her mother had insisted on after Rouenna's brother Thad crashed his motorcycle into a bridge pylon on his way home from a party one wet dawn. This happened about two years after Rouenna returned from Vietnam, and if anything could bring it all back it was the sight of that boy's battered body (he hadn't been wearing a helmet when he crashed and was said to have been doing ninety) laid out in the hospital morgue. For a while, before she met her second husband, Rouenna's mother had lived with her youngest, Henry, in a winterized bungalow at the Shore. With remarriage had come this old house, a handsome, solidly built Colonial on a quiet, pleasant street dense with shade trees, the house where her second husband had grown up. She had been happy with her second husband, a car dealer as handsome and solid and square as the house. When he died of cancer, Rouenna had feared that her mother would lapse into her old pattern of drinking and sleeping her days away. Instead, Teresa LoPresto (she had taken her new husband's name) began taking courses at a beauty institute in Trenton and got a license as an electrologist, followed by a job in a salon at one of the new malls. She redecorated the house. She never stopped taking care of herself, not even during the worst days of her grief, she quit smoking (it was cancer of the lung that had killed her husband, and in quitting she granted his dying wish), and as soon as she was out of mourning she began to date. Not young anymore, she had never lost her interest in or her ability to attract men. And in every way her middle years were turning out to be happier than her youth. Like many women of her generation, she had married too young, to the first—the only—boy she'd ever kissed, she had started having babies right out of her teens. Slowly, slowly the years rolled by, all the time in the world to get to know her prison, and no escape that she could detect, unless you counted losing her mind. But she was not like those women you were forever hearing about these days, doomed to repeat the same stupid mistake their whole lives. After her first husband died, she steered clear of men who were like him, and though from time to time she might date trouble, because trouble could be hot, trouble could be fun once in a while, when it came to marriage she looked for the stable, the reliable, the kind. The way

Rouenna put it to Henry: "I think maybe Mom has finally grown up." Rouenna saw it as a consequence of all those deaths: a mother, a father, two husbands, a son—nothing like death to make a person grow up. It happened all the time during the war, only a lot faster. A single firefight could do it. One shift on the emergency ward.

And now Teresa LoPresto was about to become Teresa McFaye. She had met her fiancé through a dating service for "mature" Catholic singles. A widower, a retired fire captain, a former marine who, like Rouenna's father, was a World War II veteran who'd fought in Okinawa, he was old-fashioned. He would not have them living together before they were wed. In another month this would be their house, their room, their bed.

And when was the last time Rouenna's mother had spoken of Rouenna's father? Rouenna could not recall. It was almost as if that first marriage, that entire period of her mother's life, had never happened. She had shoved it deep, she had buried it under heaps of coal. The place where it lay was a place where rats roamed and seagulls cried and foghorns blew, guarded by the ghost of King. (Always the sight of a German shepherd—hard to avoid on any army base—could fill Rouenna with pain.)

Her mother's bedroom: pretty, clean, nothing like the rooms where Rouenna had grown up. Roach would have to take the bus to get here. Outside the window the dogwood blossomed, lilting with a breeze, the shadow of a branch pawing at the bedroom wall, like Gigi at the door when she wanted to go out. For an instant sunlight pierced the clouds and was met with a burst of ecstatic birdsong.

Rouenna lay motionless on her mother's bed. It was as if a gas had seeped from that heart-shaped box. With an effort she could have roused herself, but did she really want to? It had been a long time since she had done this much thinking about the past. And it was not some horrific flashback she was experiencing but that indescribable mixture of joy and anguish and longing that only Vietnam was able to produce in her.

"Where would you like to go, lieutenant?"

What a question. She hadn't expected to be asked, and she had no answer. She did not know one part of Vietnam from another. All she'd been hoping was to avoid the one or two hospitals where instead of fatigues nurses had to wear white. She told the assignments officer she didn't care where she was stationed but if possible she would rather not be stuck in the same place for her whole tour always doing the same thing. The assignments officer had not been able to resist: "Afraid you'll get bored?" But Rouenna's wish was easily granted. After six months in Danang (and two weeks' R and R in Hong Kong), she would find herself back down-country at another evac hospital, in Long Binh. Between the two hospitals, she would be assigned at different times to work on the receiving ward, the postoperative and intensive care unit, the medical unit, and the Vietnamese unit. She would also put in time helping to train Vietnamese nurses at a civilian clinic, a poor tumbledown place (like most Vietnamese hospitals, it was far inferior to the Long Binh Military Dog Hospital) that immediately brought back a film she had seen as a kid, in school, about sick natives in Africa, and that teacher who hated her, now what was her name, rhymed with *bitch.* Not that Rouenna could recall any teacher who had ever really liked her. She had never been a good student. Even in nursing school, which she hated, as she hated all school, she had been near the bottom of her class. It was only in Vietnam that she became what

she had never been before: a quick study. Of course, you learned
more in a month in the combat zone than you did in a year in any
stateside hospital. (One of the few things Rouenna had been told
before coming to Nam that would turn out to be completely
true.) A nurse on these wards would see things that she would
never see anywhere else. Many of the skills she acquired on her
tour she would never use again. Besides the gamut of combat
wounds, Rouenna now saw cases of malaria, dengue fever,
typhoid, dysentery, bubonic plague, tuberculosis, and cholera.
Leprosy, and other skin diseases that had no scientific name: the
creeping crud, this-or-that rot. Jungle foot and jungle crotch.
Snake bites, insect bites almost as bad as snake bites. Other bites,
too, monkey, dog, human, rat. Rabies. Worms, leeches, scabies,
lice. Heatstroke, combat fatigue, monsoon madness. VD, *beau-
coup* VD—supposedly you could get the Purple Heart for a bad
case of VD. Never a penis that had run into a razor blade. (But
once, most memorably, a head that had run into chopper blades.)
Bored? You never knew what it might be next. Short-timer syn-
drome escalating into psychosis. The new guy who made it only
as far as the replacement depot when his appendix ruptured. ("I
ain't fakin'! I swear I ain't fakin'!") The tainted beans and dicks
that felled a platoon. Bottle cuts and busted heads sustained in a
race riot. Drunks needing to have their stomachs pumped. The
recon scout ambushed by a tiger. A boy brought in from the field
dead but without a scratch (aneurysm). The Green Beret captain
diagnosed with leukemia. ("Now ain't that a kick in the nuts.") A
general come to the recovery room to distribute medals keeling
over with a heart attack. A Victoria Charlie, breasts pocked with
cigarette burns, giving birth to twins so small you could hold
both of them in one hand. Stillbirths.

"You know, you couldn't make this shit up." He was a corps-man named Luciano. "*Un*lucky" Luciano—because he was one of those army sad sacks who seemed never to be able to do anything right and was forever catching hell. He was helping Rouenna to go through the effects of an unidentified soldier she had just prepped for surgery. The kid was expected to live, but he would never be the same. Now it turned out he'd been collecting the same body part he himself had just lost to a bouncing betty mine. "The worst, man," *Un*lucky kept saying. "The absolute fucking worst."

Before the war the worst thing Rouenna had ever seen was a baby that was born with no eyes. She remembered the sound—the collective gasp in the delivery room when the infant's head appeared—and how it was all anyone at the hospital could talk about for weeks. The missing eyes turned out to be just one of many things wrong with that baby. In Vietnam Rouenna sometimes used the eyeless baby as a measure. At least these are grown-ups, she would tell herself. At least they've had a chance to live some normal years, see some good things in life, have a little fun. An attempt at perspective that she thought would help keep her sane but that could be taken only so far. For one thing, among the most horrendous casualties she had seen were two seventeen-year-old high school dropouts, and she'd heard of boys as young as fifteen who had lied about their age and got their boyish wish to come fight this war. Among the Vietnamese on both sides were soldiers as young or even younger than that, and everywhere you looked you saw children—indisputably children—with the same terrible wounds and lopped limbs as the injured combatants. Hysterical mothers brought hopelessly maimed kids to the military emergency rooms. Desperately ill and disabled kids were left abandoned at all the bases. Once, in a shoebox, a malnourished infant that survived only hours. Whenever they had the time, doctors and nurses would drive off base to bring medical care and supplies to villagers. On one such Medcap mission, to an orphanage outside Hue, the first thing Rouenna saw was a nun holding a baby with a hideously scarred face. The nun made a beeline for her, and with a toothy welcoming smile thrust that baby girl, whose eyes had been destroyed by shrapnel, into Rouenna's shaking hands.

Medcaps was one thing, a good thing, even if some of those villagers' hearts and minds belonged to the other side, even if many of the donated supplies ended up on the black market or in enemy hands. But like everyone else, Rouenna balked at treating prisoners of war. Turn away from our boys suffering and dying in all those beds to help the very bastards who had put them there? Why on earth would you do it? Because you were ordered to. What made Rouenna feel even more disloyal was the admiration that grew in spite of herself. Not that the Americans were not stoic, god knows they were—the marines in particular were forever proving their grit. But there was something about the way the Vietnamese bore up—not just the POWs but the civilians, even the women, even some of the children—that struck everybody. The silence of those wards—who hadn't been spooked by it? One MP assigned to guard prisoners said, "It just goes to prove, they don't feel pain same as we do"—a wellworn explanation. That guard was on duty one night during Rouenna's shift. She had just finished changing a dressing on an NVA soldier's leg, avoiding his eyes the whole time (she knew he was scowling viciously). Only at the last minute she happened to glance into his face, and he spat at her. When she cried out, the MP came flying over and brought the butt of his M-16 down into the man's gut several times. Not a moan. "See what I mean?" The MP walked back to his post, shaking his head in disgust. "We ain't never gonna win this fucking war."

For Rouenna, the amazing thing was how fast it had happened. As if the man hadn't even thought about what he was doing. It was like instinct on his part, the spit bursting from his lips the instant Rouenna glanced at him, as if to ward off evil. To be so instinctively hated by someone she didn't know, someone to whom she had done nothing but good—this was strange, and hard. She might not have wanted to treat NVAs or VCs, but when she had to she did it right, giving the same treatment she would have given anyone. Other nurses she knew handled prisoners roughly, took their sizable rage and frustration out on them and made no bones about it. She knew of surgical teams that were less than fastidious about scrubbing before procedures on prisoners, cases where painkillers or antibiotics or even sometimes anesthetics had been withheld. Rouenna had a superstitious streak like her mother. She believed that if she broke her oath, if she gave in to the temptation to hurt someone, she would get hurt herself. *An eye for an eye* was not just an expression here, either—think of that boy and his souvenirs. And there were so many ways you could get hurt in Vietnam.

The burn on the NVA's thigh was a bad one. Rouenna had been very gentle changing the dressing and scrupulous about minimizing the risk of infection. She had respected the soldier's dignity and privacy and tried to avoid eye contact to make the whole business less hard on him. And the goddamn motherfucking gook bastard had spat at her.

She got over it. It was the only way—*no sensitive plants!* But it wasn't easy taking care of the man after that. To buck herself up and to annoy him as much as possible, when she changed his dressing or his IV bottle now, she would sing very loud and off key: "The Star-Spangled Banner" and "Yankee Doodle Dandy." Now, that made him wince. Sometimes he would say something to her. There were interpreters around the hospital, but Rouenna didn't really need one.

"Well, Prince Charles, one of the only Vietnamese phrases they taught me how to say is 'I'm sorry,' but I guess no one ever taught you, huh?"

It was a relief when that major was well enough to be transferred to the POW compound, where Rouenna figured there was even a chance he might start to appreciate her.

And when the time came to tell the history of the Vietnam War and to reckon all the mistakes the U.S. Army made, would anyone remember Polly?

Polly, Pretty Polly. Her real name was Helga. Helga Paulina di Venere. Polly. That the army had recruited her at all was unthinking enough. To have sent her to Nam was unconscionable. It was as if no one anywhere along the line had ever looked up from the paperwork.

In the words of one overexcited PFC: "It's like Ann-Margret and Gina Lollobrigida mushed together." The boy had an eye at least. Polly was half Swedish, half Italian. She even spoke some Swedish, which was about as useful in Vietnam as everything else about her.

Here, where even the plainest janes attracted as much attention as any leggy, large-breasted, beautiful blonde, send in one leggy, large-breasted, beautiful blonde.

Constantly being goggled at, being followed around, constantly having your picture taken—this was part of every army nurse's life. Hoots and hollers, whistles, applause. Now and then the attention might pitch over into harassment and there were always one or two peeping toms, but for the most part civility—even chivalry—prevailed. But with Polly came an element of chaos. It was like the time a rumor arose that the real Ann-Margret was coming to visit, and the men were almost beside themselves. As it happened, it was not Ann-Margret (such rumors were frequent and frequently wrong) but a different sexpot, who came all right but took one look at all those double and triple amps and fled. *Cunt*, one furious nurse spat after her. The men were crushed, but it was not the only disappointment of its kind; not everyone can be Martha Raye. As for the nurses, they were never too pleased about the female celebrities and entertainers who occasionally breezed through. Some were outright jealous over the fuss. After all, what did those glamour pusses do for the men compared with the nurses?

But what about Polly—nurse, glamour puss, and second lieutenant all "mushed together," and not breezing through? She could not relax at the officers' club or shop at the PX without being mobbed. Her commission was about as much protection as a cheerleader's skirt in a cartwheel. GIs turned cartwheels themselves whenever she appeared. Superiors ordered her to drink and dine and dance with them. Her presence was commanded at places no other lowly lieutenant would ever be asked.

She was a celebrity herself, Pretty Polly was. And, like everything else about the army and Vietnam, she hated it.

"They told me I'd be going to Germany. They told me there was no way I could ever end up in Vietnam unless I wanted to go, which I made perfectly clear I did not want. *I can't believe I'm here!* When I got my orders, I wasn't even upset at first, because I knew there'd been a mistake. I went to the chief nurse"— distorting her features into as ugly a smirk as those features could make—"'Sorry, lieutenant, the army doesn't make that kind of mistake.'" (This story was getting old.)

Two things Pretty Polly cared about in life: her Irish setter and her handsome big brother (both "Red"), and they were both home in Minneapolis. She had their pictures all over the hooch. All she could think about was getting back to them. Prettiest round-eye in all of Nam, and no interest whatsoever in romance. This gave rise to the rumor that she was a lesbian—another well-worn explanation (and a rampant rumor about military women in general). Rouenna knew that this was not it—but what the hell was it? She herself found it hard not to fall in love at least once a week, had to use all her control not to spend every minute off duty in the bush-tanned arms of one warrior or another. ("Come on, baby, tomorrow we're going out on patrol, you know I could die out there." "That's what your buddy said." "What do you want me to say?" "Don't say anything, just kiss me.") It would have been different if Polly had a boyfriend back home she was saving herself for, but she told Rouenna there was no one. It made Rouenna start to wonder about that big brother.

Having Polly for a hoochmate was a trial and a half. She was a sensitive plant. She was as homesick as it was possible for any human being to be, she was in tears much of the time. She could not resign herself to the fate, the dirty trick that had landed her in the middle of a war. ("I was just looking for a little help paying for school!") Last thing in the world she was up for was the challenge of combat nursing. As a student she had dreamed of one day finding a job as a nurse in a fancy private school—the extent of her career ambition. Not a mistake but a terrible wrong had brought Polly to Vietnam, and she was not going to make the best of it. Even the lesser hardships—annoyances such as the heat, the mildew, the bugs, the cold showers, and the outdoor latrines—Polly would never get used to. (Though even going to the latrine was not the simple event for her that it was for everyone else, at least not since someone had sneaked in and scratched in the back of the door: "Dear Lt. di V. This soldier would eat a mile of your shit just to see where it came from.")

Nausea, gagging—even seasoned nurses sometimes had trouble, especially with the burn victims. But Polly was the only one who often had to run from the room.

"A squeamish nurse. Just what we need around here." This time it *did* get said: by Rouenna.

Polly was squeamish about maggots, too, and maggots—well, there was no escaping the maggots.

Something had happened while Polly was still stateside finishing up basic training, something she had not shaken by the time she arrived. She and a buddy had gone off base for some burgers and fries. The buddy went in to get the food while she stayed with the jeep, stepping out just to stretch her long legs. They were on her almost before she saw them, punching, kicking, knocking her down. Armed with squeeze-bottles, they smeared her with ketchup: uniform, face, hair. "That's Vietnamese blood, you cunt, you fucking army cunt, that's what you want, isn't it, you fucking pig." At the time, Polly still believed she was going to Germany. The kids had jumped in their van and driven away before her buddy came out and found her. Two days later, Polly got her orders for Nam.

One of the hottest, most challenging and dangerous places in-country a nurse could find herself stationed was Pleiku. So Pleiku is where the army sends Pretty Polly first. At the time she arrives, the compound is under constant attack. The incoming wounded never stop, all hands are needed around the clock. When a break comes at last, sleep is unthinkable: the noise, the fear. Soon Polly is good for almost nothing: hard to thread a suture when your hands won't stop shaking. Sleepless, she can barely stand. She refuses the Dex everyone else is popping. (One other thing that sets Polly apart: she does not smoke, drink to excess, or take drugs. What is she *doing* here? people said.) She weeps, she tears her blond hair, she begs to be allowed to go home. ("Or at least let me go like they promised to Germany!") Instead she is transferred to Long Binh. Not Frankfurt, but relatively safe. She and Rouenna arrive at the hospital the same week. By now Rouenna is halfway through her tour, she has passed her hump day, she has been promoted to first lieutenant, she has treated hundreds of patients and become a combat nurse of considerable skill. Polly is still in every way very much a new guy, with ten months of duty to go. But the more important distinction is this: Rouenna belongs, Polly does not.

Except for a couple of doctors and hospital administrators, lifers—the REMFs (rear echelon motherfuckers) that *everyone* hated—Rouenna got along with the people she met in the army, and she had never enjoyed being with anyone as much as she enjoyed being with the friends she made during the war. Some said it was all the bad times, the grueling work, the endless horror and heartbreak, that made the good times so rewarding. Others said it was the premium pot. Whatever it was, Rouenna never laughed so hard, she never had so much fun as she had that year in Vietnam. And here was another surprise: the people she bonded tightest with were other women. Sisterhood: this was new to Rouenna. The only girl in her family, she'd been a tomboy up until high school. (The day she walked into a drugstore to buy sanitary napkins for the first time, the man at the counter looked up and said, "Can I help you, son?") Older, she developed a fear of other girls, especially the popular ones, who were snotty and cutthroat and for whom she did not exist. And it wasn't that she was completely friendless, but she knew that whoever had scrawled "Weirdo" and "Loser" on her school locker was not expressing just one person's opinion. Getting sick with mono and then being left back had not helped. Not friendless, but something of a loner, not one to share much in school social life, that's how she was. Certainly she had never known anything like the closeness she would find in the Army Nurse Corps, nor would she ever find such closeness again. Home from the war, she would be struck by how hard it was all of a sudden to make friends with other women. There was her having been to the war in the first place, which was mystifying, not to say off-putting, to every woman she knew (including her mother, who had not wanted Rouenna to go but had looked on the bright side: "At least it's not one of my boys"). A female Vietnam veteran: it was Weirdo and Loser all over again. But her being a vet was not the only barrier. It seemed to Rouenna there was always something in the way between women as there had been something in the way between teenage girls. It might be rivalry, or a lack of trust; something that made you wary. It might have had to do with how critical most women were, especially of other women. At any rate, back in the world, the camaraderie she had taken for granted in Nam was impossible even to imagine.

She would always look back dreamily to the hours she spent with the other nurses, off duty, drinking or smoking grass and listening to music. She remembered thinking that this must be what college was like, roommates in a dorm, sorority sisters. Now and then, when they had all had enough of parties and had seen the Clint Eastwood movie that was playing on base two or three times, when they needed a break from dating and just wanted some time by themselves, they would declare a Girl Night. They would put on their beloved Motown records, turning the volume up louder and louder as the night wore on. They would give one another shampoos and pedicures and back rubs. They would break out the brownies or banana bread someone's mother had sent, and the opium-laced Marlboros they had bought from the hooch maid, Van. They would tell stories and dirty jokes, getting higher and higher, shrieking and egging one another on. One night they all ended up dancing together wearing only their helmets and jungle boots. They posed for snapshots like that, though they knew they would never have the nerve to get them developed anywhere in-country. "We could be court-martialed!" "Hey, let's do it then—they'll have to send us home!"

It was on another night, at a farewell party for one of the pilots, sitting on the floor between two guys with whom she was sharing a joint, that Rouenna had the following thoughts: I am happy. I am not faking. I am not putting on an act or a brave front, I am not way down inside all in knots wondering if everyone at this party likes me. I know that everyone likes me, just as I like them. I have never been this happy. This smile on my face is real.

And she knew: burnt out from nursing as she was, and sick as she was of the carnage, and loud as she might sing "We Gotta Get Out of This Place" when everyone else did, and much as she might mean it, she was going to miss Vietnam. At her own farewell party, she would be sad. It gave her pain even now. This was not the kind of experience you could share with people who hadn't been here, too. Those who came back to Vietnam after having been in the States for a while all broadcast the same warning: Don't expect a warm welcome home, and don't expect anyone to know what the fuck you're talking about.

Hardest of all would be to explain why she had been so *happy.*

Every time someone rotated out, there was a party, and at every one of these parties addresses were exchanged and promises to stay in touch were made, but of course everyone knew that this was not the way things usually turned out. And anyway no reunion could ever be the same, the unique magical trip they had going here would vanish completely once they were gone, and whatever friendships, old or new, they might have back in the world would never be this intense—everyone knew that. It was yet another kind of loss that you faced as a veteran. And sitting on the floor with her two friends, Rouenna wondered how it was possible to be so stoned and so clearheaded at the same time. She did not think she had ever been so clearheaded in her entire life. She was sure she had never been given such a startling vision, as if someone had handed her a crystal ball in which she saw herself many years from now, a woman sitting alone in a strange room, a shadow moving on the wall, holding pieces of a heart. A woman thinking these thoughts. And taking the joint that had come back to her (was that *all* the time that had passed? the time it took for two people each to take one hit?), and raising her voice to be heard above the music, Rouenna said, "Man, this is some powerful shit!"

But where in all this did Pretty Polly fit? She did not even try. She avoided the parties as she avoided the officers' club. Otherwise, she would have had no peace. She was too angry, anyway, too bitter and too scared to relax for one minute in-country. And she was no admirer of soldiers. She saw a lot of the GIs as pure brutes. (That's what came of their relentless attempts to impress her, to prove with all their gory stories just what mad, bad, born-to-kill motherfucking warriors they were.) Like Rouenna, she had not had any opinion about the war before she arrived. But now she could see for herself how evil it was, and she could not wait to go home and tell people. (Not that she was the only member of the military in-country against the war; it was getting so you had to look far to find someone who wasn't.) Meanwhile, back in Minneapolis, her brother had become involved in the protest movement and was using the letters she wrote home to feed the flames.

Though doctors still found every excuse to brush or push up against her, their patience with Polly was wearing thin. Most people who had to work with her felt some resentment, and not just for her lack of skill. "Lieutenant, the next time a dying GI asks you to hold his hand and you pull away like that, I will personally kick the living daylights out of you."

She often cried on *Un*lucky's shoulder.

"I just wish I could *do* something for her, man," he said.

Rouenna wished the same—but what could they do? "Unlucky" would have fit Polly, too. That weak stomach, for one thing. You just never knew. There were budding doctors who were forced to change careers when they discovered to their own surprise that they were too susceptible to nausea or fainting. (The army would have sent them to Vietnam.) It would have to be Polly, of course, who lost a contact lens in a sucking chest wound, whose purse was snatched on a visit to Saigon, and who, on that same visit, was knocked down by a moped—on purpose, she insisted, describing the driver's backward look of spiteful glee as he sped on. (To the Vietnamese, of course, Polly was no heart-stilling goddess but just another hulking big-nosed American whose body smells were as sharp as a dog's and who broke chairs just by sitting in them.)

One day, when they had been about a month at Long Binh, Polly, who would not have dreamed of going to the PX alone, asked Rouenna to go with her, and Rouenna, who had some shopping to do herself, said yes.

As usual, the PX was crowded with GIs who reacted to the women's appearance with the usual stir, to which the women responded with the usual feigned nonchalance.

Men fell in behind them as they headed for toiletries.

"Shit," said Polly, scanning the shelves. "No tampons—just like Pleiku."

Like Pleiku and everywhere else in-country; it was one of the nurses' many little frustrations. Not even the black market could help. The Vietnamese maids looked at you as if you were mad. Jade earrings, Vietcong flags, and "any kind drug you want, babysan." But tampons? Forget about it.

"What are we supposed to do?"

Rouenna knew that Polly knew the answer to that question as well as she did: get your mother to send some.

"I thought it might be different here," Polly said. "I mean, this place is so big." A great big PX on a great big base, the biggest military base in Vietnam. Tens of thousands of Americans were stationed at Long Binh. Long Binh, U.S.A.: a large but tamponless American town in the heart of Southeast Asia.

Polly's voice was too loud. A couple of privates standing close by were eating it up, laughing and elbowing each other's ribs. Rouenna sighed. Some of these guys.

"Don't sweat this, Polly. I've got a box back in my room. And they might have some at the PX in Saigon."

But, as if she hadn't heard a word, Polly went on: "This place is so fucking big. They've got everything here. They've got TV sets and stereo sets and radios, they've got cameras, they've got food and clothes and booze and cigarettes." It was true. Somehow, they had it all. Golf clubs. Fountain pens. Watches. Chess sets. One of the nurses wore a diamond engagement ring from the PX. You could buy a pizza or a motorcycle or a mink stole. Rouenna herself had bought a guitar. There was even a toy section, where Rouenna had once seen a Barbie doll lying facedown with her head in a GI Joe's lap. "They've got fucking *surfboards—*"

"Be cool," Rouenna said sharply. "What else do you need from here? *And lower your goddamn voice.*" Rouenna had no intention of being part of an even bigger spectacle than they already were. But Polly—again as if she had not heard a word—started walking away. What the hell was she up to? Moving so fast, people had to jump back. Heading for the exit, Rouenna presumed as she hurried to catch up. But as they turned a corner, Polly stopped.

"Oh, look. *Here's* some women's stuff."

Rouenna winced. Lingerie. Yes, the PX sold women's lingerie, everyone knew that. What the hell was this crazy bitch up to? Plucking at a negligee on display, rubbing the black gauze between finger and thumb. Where did she think she was— Macy's?

"Couldn't hide much under there, now, could we. Perfect for these hot tropical nights. Oooh—and look over here: *fishnet stockings.* My, my, doesn't this man's army think of everything. Why, I'll bet they've even got crotchless panties around here somewhere. What do you think?"

What Rouenna was thinking was how peculiar Polly had begun to look. Gray, except for two uneven bright splotches like drunkenly applied blush on her cheeks. There was a sheen of moisture over her skin, but her lips were dry and unnaturally pale. Rouenna was thinking that Polly looked exactly the way she looked just before she had to run from the room. Rouenna half expected her to bolt right then. Instead she raised her voice and went on: "Amazing, isn't it, how the army remembers to stock these things. For the boys. For their little gook whores. But can't manage to get tampons or sanitary napkins for the nurses."

If there hadn't been a crowd watching, Rouenna told the other nurses later, it would have been easy. "I would have slapped her across the mouth and dragged her out by the hair." But there was a crowd, and they could not have been watching more intently. All laughing and rib-poking had ceased. At Polly's last words, a ripple passed through the men as everyone shifted his weight. There was a noise like the *whoosh* of distant artillery. Most of the men continued to stare, frowning, hands on hips, but a few had turned away or were looking down at their feet. A mutter from somewhere at the back: "—the fuck she talking about?" No one moved. At last Rouenna found her command voice. "Okay, lieutenant, start walking, don't stop before we get to the exit, and keep your mouth shut, you hear? Not another fucking word about tampons."

"Affirm. Not a word about tampons." Polly was now talking in a hoarse stage whisper. "Shhh. Let's forget about tampons. I'll just bleed. I'll bleed all over this fucking place. I mean, what's a little more blood in this fucking place. That's all we see around here anyway, is fucking blood. Who's going to notice a little more blood? Blood, blood, blood, blood, blood." With each "blood" a bubble of saliva that had formed between Polly's lips enlarged slightly. Then she hiccupped, and the bubble burst. She bent far forward at the waist, her head almost touching her shins, and when she straightened up again—it was almost like some kind of dance step, Rouenna explained later—she threw back her head and cackled.

For Rouenna, the next fifteen minutes—the time it took to get Polly out of there—were as bad as any fifteen minutes she would spend in Vietnam. Inching along, her heart in her throat, the hairs on the back of her neck erect—it was like moving over ground you knew might be mined. She had to agree with the men who said it would have been easier if one of them carried Polly, but instinct told her Polly would start screaming if any of them touched her. They were all somber and solicitous now, the men—now that they knew what they were seeing, having seen it before, most of them, though never before in a woman.

Outside, the sky was almost black, and it was raining Vietnamese style: from every direction. By the time they got back to their quarters, the women were soaked through. It was not until Polly reached her own room that she appeared to recognize where she was, and that is when she started screaming, waking all the night nurses who'd been trying to sleep. One of them threw on a poncho and dashed to the hospital for a syringe and a vial of Librium. Rouenna stayed with Polly until she was out. Then, early in the day though it was, she took herself a few doors down to the officers' club. She was breaking her own rule, never to drink this close to the start of her shift, but then like most everyone else she drank so much off duty she knew she could handle it, even on an empty stomach, three vodka and tonics, chug, chug, chug, no sweat.

Silver lining: Polly woke from her crisis a different person. It was as if traces of the Librium remained in her system. She was calmer, more efficient on duty, more relaxed off. So: she was going to make it through her tour after all. She even let Rouenna drag her to a couple of parties. But she still would not date. Most of these guys, she told Rouenna, were not her type. Rouenna didn't get it. As far as she could see, every type was here, from West Coast beach boy to Staten Island hood. Except for the wimps and the spit-shined ass-kissers, they were all her type, she confessed. Polly teased her. "Lieutenant, you're the kind of girl that gives army women a bad name."

Was Polly a virgin? Was that it? Polly laughed and shook her head. Then how did she do it? Look around: every male heartthrob was right here on this base. Troy Donahue, James Dean, Tab Hunter, Richard Chamberlain, Sal Mineo, Warren Beatty,

Steve McQueen. And Polly could have had her pick! Polly could have had them all! Again, Rouenna found herself wondering about that big brother.

And here was another cause for wonder: How could anyone as pretty as Polly care so little about her own looks? Without a doubt she was the least conceited girl Rouenna had ever met.

The two women are together one day when they run into a unit returning to base from the field. The men are the usual sight: blear-eyed, gaunt-cheeked, filthy, and dazed, hardly aware of anything around them. Then one mud-caked kid glances their way and sees Polly. He stops, shakes his head a few times as if to clear it, then comes staggering over, eyes never leaving her face, and when he is standing right in front of her he gets down on his knees. Never says a word. It is the kind of thing that happens to Polly all the time, the kind of thing she hates. She turns and walks away, leaving Rouenna to think how if it were she— if she, Rouenna, had that kind of power—she would not be able to resist using it. Like a whip she would use it. To get things—to get whatever she wanted. To make people dance attendance on her. To make people sorry. No doors or curtains in the women's shower room, so Rouenna has seen the full range of her buddy's arsenal, and she knows that if she had anything like what Polly has she would use it every day of her life, use it as she has seen so many beautiful women do. Use it to bring people to their knees.

These were not thoughts to be proud of, and Rouenna knew it, and so Polly's behavior seemed to her not just wondrous but a sign of good character. She's a better person than I am, Rouenna sometimes thought. It did not make her like Polly less.

———

It was Rouenna who talked Polly into volunteering for Medcaps. "It's good to get away from this place for a day, and it's a nice change of pace."

This particular mission was to a village between Saigon and Cu Chi. They would leave after breakfast and be back before dangerous dark, one doctor, two nurses, one corpsman, and of course the mandatory guards. One of the drivers was a kid from Oklahoma City who had the same kind of spectacular good looks that Polly had. They called him Johnny Angel, and he had been in-country just a few weeks. To see him and Pretty Polly together was to think this must be a movie being made about the war, with these two the leads. Only fitting they should ride in the same jeep.

When they stopped at the gate, the MP glared at Johnny Angel with malevolent envy. Johnny Angel adjusted his dark sunglasses and flashed the widest, brightest movie-star grin, a grin that said, Hell, this war ain't all bad, now is it?

"I Binh down so Long," sang Rags the corpsman, as the jeep bearing him and Rouenna followed through the gate. And though she had heard it a thousand times before, Rouenna laughed. She was in good spirits, too. Everyone usually was, setting out on Medcaps. They would spend the day deworming, delousing, vaccinating, and dressing sores, and compared with their usual workday it was a lark. And it really was good to get off base. Medcaps was an exception to the rule prohibiting travel in jeeps or choppers by medical staff, who were considered too valuable to put at risk—one of many rules that was constantly broken, and Rouenna couldn't say which tickled her more, breaking the rule or being called valuable. Long Binh was all concrete and wire and corrugated metal, not a patch of nonarmy green in sight. In fact, it *could* have been a movie set, something that had gone up fast and would come down faster (not a stick of it stands today). People compared it to a space station somewhere, not planet Earth. No trees, no birds—people said it reminded them of *The Twilight Zone.* But whatever it reminded you of, you were always happy to get away from the noisy, stinking, dirty shithole of a place. And when you drove into the surrounding country-side, you couldn't help being dazzled by the glowing green of the ricefields, refreshed by the lush green smell.

"Hey, Rags," said Rouenna, continuing the game. "How Long has it Binh since you smelled grass?"

"How Long has it Binh since you smoked some?"

There were Vietnamese on the road, some on foot and some on bicycles, some pushing carts, and it was not always easy maneuvering around them. The jeep drivers honked and honked. There were Vietnamese in the fields as well, farmers at work. Usually these people ignored any Americans passing by, but today everyone seemed in good spirits, Vietnamese too, and when the Americans waved to them they waved back cheerfully. They waved and called or signaled to others farther along the road, so that when the jeeps appeared those Vietnamese also paused in their hoeing to watch and to wave cheerfully. They waved cheerfully, distractingly, and the sharpshooter among them raised his hoe to his shoulder, took aim, and fired.

Polly felt something like a bee stinging her cheek. Then Johnny Angel's sunglasses flew into her lap, and the stung side of her face and neck were all wet.

Immediately the guards started spraying the paddy, shooting at the little figures escaping at almost cartoonish speed over the dikes.

One doctor, two nurses, and one corpsman could not save Johnny Angel. Driving back to the base, they had the road all to themselves. Every Vietnamese, every bicycle and cart, had vanished. The fields were empty. There was nothing but a lone buffalo, and so the guards shot it, pumping it with enough bullets to bring down a herd.

Afterward the usual things got said. No one was safe anywhere in Nam, being on the road was a risk even in daylight, which was the reason for armed guards in the first place. Lucky for the survivors it was just a sniper this time and not an ambush. Medcaps was bullshit, these fucking villagers were all fucking VC, Medcaps was aid and comfort to the enemy. Johnny Angel, aged twenty, worth ten dinks any day, and now look. All you could do was go out and kill ten dinks for him.

Polly wrote a letter to Johnny Angel's parents, telling them how he had died. She explained that he had been killed instantly and that he had not suffered. She described the last moments of his life, relaxed and pleasant moments, during which he and she had been making small talk, about where they were from, and how many brothers and sisters they each had. She recorded his last words: "Oh, man, you gotta visit Oklahoma sometime."

To Rouenna she said, "We volunteered for that mission, you and I, but that boy did not volunteer. Because we wanted to go to that village that boy was ordered to drive us there. We are responsible."

And: "It wasn't even for anything important, either. He was in that jeep with me because I was going to help people I don't even know or care about. I just wanted to get off base for the day, like you said. I just wanted *a change of pace*."

Rouenna said, "And what the fuck do you think we can do about it now?"

"I don't care what you do. But I can't stay here anymore. I'm getting out."

There was no farewell party for Polly, but a few days before she was to fly home she and Rouenna hitched a ride together to Saigon. They were not supposed to leave the base, but getting men to cooperate in sneaking past the MPs was never hard. What was hard was convincing the men that until it was time to go back the women would not want an escort. They had plans, a quiet dinner together. ("You mean, you two want to be alone?")

Downtown was hopping. Knots of soldiers, ARVN as well as GIs, knots of street kids, vendors, beggars, whores. The usual snarl of bikes, pedicabs, and motor vehicles. The usual noxious air. And the noise—two people walking side by side had to shout to hear each other. And on every corner somebody yelling at someone about something—a policeman at a street kid, a passenger at his cab driver, one whore at another (who gave as good as she got). Knots of spectators at each scene. A beggar missing all four limbs and wearing nothing but a pair of green U.S. Army briefs would not let go of the hem of a monk's robe that he had grasped with his teeth. Another spectacle, a group of black GIs dapping, had drawn its own large crowd. The Vietnamese had no idea what they were watching, but they were spellbound.

Dressed in civvies, strolling on Tu Do Street, ignoring stares, themselves staring plenty, Rouenna and Polly could have been tourists, were tourists to be found in that town. An army town: bar, brothel, brothel, bar, bar, bar—many of them bar and brothel in one. Some wild, shoot-'em-up saloons as good a place as any to get hurt in Vietnam. Cowboy bars. Cracker bars. Bars where neither Vietnamese nor black soldiers would ever go. At certain hours, at this hour, you could walk through downtown and hear a different kind of music, none of it Vietnamese, every few steps. A country-western singer doing "Tennessee Waltz," GIs wailing along to "Bridge Over Troubled Water," some Beatles, some Motown, some Piaf. Go-go music. A door swung open, offering a glimpse of a girl from the waist down. Black fishnet stockings and short white boots. No pubic hair.

Sometimes the music floated down from above. There were lots of rooftop clubs, especially at the hotels.

The restaurant was French, one of many Saigon restaurants where only foreigners were welcome, though the owner himself was Vietnamese. Rouenna had been there with dates a few times before. There was a patio where you could dine looking out on the Saigon River. Sometimes, on the hottest days or after heavy rain, the smell made it impossible to sit outside. At certain hours, not this hour, you might see people—only foreigners, again—waterskiing. Today there were only boats. The view stirred an ancient memory. Sampans loaded with baskets of fish and coconuts, tinkly music, natives beckoning at the camera, palm trees, bougainvillea. Vietnam. No barbed wire, no bunkers, no guard towers, no bomb craters, no fields of dust, no matchstick forests. *Vietnam*, the movie screened for nursing students by army recruiters.

Every other time she had been to this restaurant, Rouenna had ordered steak, which was what most of the customers ordered, but today the wife of the owner, who was half French and who spoke English with a French accent, urged them both to try the duck. Before the duck was served, they had bowls of cucumber soup. The soup was good, and the duck, which had been cooked with a thick fruity glaze and looked wooden and lacquered like a small violin, was superb. At first, when the woman had suggested the duck, Rouenna was skeptical, but when she tasted it she thought it must be the most delicious thing she had ever eaten. Polly liked the food as much as Rouenna did. Neither of them had ever eaten duck before. The owner's wife called it duckling. With the meal the women drank beer.

It was early for dinner—they had come early so they could get back to the base before dark. The restaurant would be crowded soon, but now there were just a few tables occupied. In one corner, eating a steak, sat another nurse from their hospital, the one who wore the diamond engagement ring from the PX. She was with her fiancé, who was also eating steak. Except for a nod when Rouenna and Polly walked in, she paid them no attention. A brave girl. She was taking the chance against which every nurse had been warned. She had given her heart to one man, and that man a line officer. When he was out in the field leading his platoon, she was at the hospital working in triage. Every time a dustoff landed, she steeled herself to ask *Which unit?* No hiding from her the many ways her man could be hurt; it was all she knew. He might be her own very next casualty. A crispy critter. A gork. Eyes, face, manhood blown away. Quadriplegic. (*Darling, I don't know how to tell you this, but I will never be able to touch you, see you, kiss you, hold you, walk with you, make love to you again.*) And would she still take that man to be her wedded husband . . . in sickness and in health, when health there would never be? He might come in so badly hit, he'd be placed immediately behind the screen with the other expectants. Or it might be all over before he came in, remains, bagged and tagged by the field medic, going straight from dustoff to graves registration. Or he might not come back at all. He might be reported missing in action, he might be a prisoner of war.

And how, oh how, would his girl carry on then?

There had been another bride-to-be, back in Danang, whose fiancé was wasted by a grenade. When the news came, she stayed calm. She held her head high. She did not break down. The next time she appeared, she had shaved off her hair. It was against regs, of course, and the hospital commander gave her hell for it. "You know what it does to the men's morale, seeing an American woman looking like a goddamn POW?" "Tell them it will grow back, sir. Unlike their arms and legs." She held her shaved head high. No one ever saw her break down.

Rouenna had lost count of all the dates she had had, she had forgotten faces, she had forgotten names. Whatever happened to most of those men she could not say. It was one other thing she had done right in Vietnam, one other skill she had learned. Have as many boyfriends as you want, love the one you're with, but don't get attached to anyone. She could have fallen madly, too, nothing simpler, but she would not. She had heeded the warning, the wise and repeated warning. Better to be the kind of girl who gave army women a bad name. Better to be like a man—she could be like a man if she had to. But she could not be like that brave girl, who rather than leave her fiancé had just extended her tour. Love. The chief nurse didn't like it at all.

"Thank you for a fabulous farewell dinner," Polly said, reaching across the table to squeeze Rouenna's hand. "You're the only thing about this place I'm going to miss." Probably she hadn't meant to say it. They had drunk a lot of beer. Poor Polly. At the moment she didn't have too many friends. She would not be leaving much good feeling behind. The rumor about her discharge was that she'd got knocked up by some REMF, one of the big brass types running the war from a Saigon villa he had all to himself.

But it wasn't true. Or rather, only the first part was true.

She didn't give a damn about the bad discharge. She said she was sure that she would never regret it. She didn't want a thing, not a fucking penny from the fucking army ever again—she had paid so dearly for what she had already taken. She and Rouenna had had the one long conversation about all this that they were ever going to have. From that conversation Rouenna had learned a word she had never heard before: *angel-maker*. Soon as she was stateside, Polly said, she would get in touch with a friend who had promised to help her. The friend knew an angel-maker. Rouenna thought of that Victoria Charlie and the two dead mice she had given birth to. The war's littlest casualties. The ones too small even to be counted.

Though it saddened her, what Polly had done and what she was going to do, Rouenna would not be sad to see the back of her. Rouenna had troubles of her own. She was short now: she had reached the final weeks of her tour. And the shorter her time, the harder some things were getting to be. In a way it was like being a new guy again: jumpy, distracted, frightened. She had not lost the sense that she was where she belonged, that she was doing a vital job and doing it well, and she clung to this. *What am I doing here?* The big question tormenting the soldiers did not have to torment her. Her mission, at least, was pure and clear.

Wasn't it. Wasn't it?

The Kentucky mountain boy with multiple gunshot wounds had been dusted off for the third time, this time just a week before he was supposed to go home. Point man, ambush. (What the hell was a kid a week short of DEROS doing walking point anyway?) Only nineteen, but he had a wife back home, a son he had never seen. He had looked so drowningly at Rouenna, dark eyes throbbing. "Elly? Where we goin'? Where they takin' me, Mama? Elly? Mama? Please stop hidin', now. *Please, please* come on out."

Later Rouenna had found herself boiling with anger at Elly and Mama—as if those poor innocent women really had done this unforgivable thing. But this was something she had picked up from the troops. The agony of being abandoned, of not being loved—it came off them like an odor mixed with the other boonie odors: sweat, exhaustion, mud, fear. They never said it straight out, of course they didn't, just as they never said *killed* or *dead* but *wasted* or *zapped* or *greased* or *caught it* or *bought it* or *blown away*. But it was always there, that other big tormenting question. *If anybody loved me, how could I be here?*

What made this one different Rouenna wasn't sure, but it was with the little mountain boy that she began to count the days that she had left in Vietnam. He had not been the first, of course, and before she went home she would see more: wounded patched up and rushed right back out to the line only to be hit again, often worse, sometimes fatally. Beclouding each time a little more the purity and clarity of her mission. Remind her again: What was she doing here?

But make no mistake, a wound could be a most wonderful, most desirable thing. Many a man prayed for it: a wound serious enough to keep him out of combat but not serious enough to mess him up for life. A million-dollar wound, the troops called it. Much discussion about how you might give yourself or a buddy such a wound. Understood, it wasn't easy. You could say Polly had one. Men tried all kinds of ways to make themselves sick. Not taking their malaria pills. Cutting themselves with dirty razors or knives. One guy pricked himself all over with a rusty nail. Another tried drinking bug juice. Still another taunted a dog until it attacked him. Rouenna lost her temper with the ones who came to her for expert advice. On the recovery wards, patients pleaded with the nurses to let them stay longer. The more desperate ones tore off dressings, reopened wounds, ripped out IVs, even broke casts. Some refused to take food or medicines in the hopes of preventing healing. The word *coward* got thrown around a lot. But Rouenna couldn't help thinking of stories about animals gnawing off their own legs to escape steel traps.

Sorrier and sorrier: that was how she would honestly have to describe the troops as she saw them. All you had to do was listen to them talk about the enemy. The night belongs to the Cong, everyone said. Because the Cong could see in the dark. Even the jungle dark, even the pitch-black tunnel dark. But even in the bright light of day, you could not see him. The Cong didn't need to eat except maybe a cup of rice every two weeks. Even in the worst heat, he could get by on a drop of water. The Cong didn't feel pain, the Cong didn't bleed the way we did. (The Cong didn't die, Rouenna was waiting to hear next.) The Cong was getting everyone more and more jittery. This was as true of officers as it was of draftees. Medics were handing out tranquilizers like mints. But there was a need for stronger stuff. First a few beds, then whole wards would be required just for the addicts. (And it was not just GIs. Rouenna wasn't at all surprised when she found that the thighs of a surgeon she was caressing were all nubby from where he'd been shooting up. Damn mosquitoes, he joked. She had her own addictions to worry about, all that alcohol, all that pot, the cigarettes she had been smoking since high school, which this year had become a three-pack-a-day habit.) Not a bad idea: get strung out, and they would have to send you home. You could always get clean once you were stateside. Bad discharge *so fucking what*. (And when the military began mandatory drug tests, they would provide yet another way out: borrow some piss from a junkie, plenty around. So the flights bearing junkies away from the war became known as golden-flow flights.)

There were those who were faking insanity and there were those who truly were too insane to be let loose (though a lot of them were) with weapons. Even the sane ended up doing insane things, like mailing enemy body parts to folks back home. And there was the other war, between white and black. Even the nurses caught some of it. A blood with hepatitis glared at Rouenna with a hatred as fierce as any prisoner of war's. "They should have more sisters to take care of the brothers here. We don't want no honky bitch touching us." The bedpan he hurled only just missed her.

Confederate flags flew from some army vehicles and were displayed in certain barracks and bars.

All this was bad, but there was worse. American soldiers in cahoots with Vietnamese gangsters, American soldiers working as pimps. Graffiti told the story: FUCK THE ARMY. FUCK NIXON. UNCLE SAM SUCKS. FRAG THE BRASS. You saw these words scrawled everywhere. You saw increased instances of troops refusing orders, of officers injured or blown away by their own men. Brain-dead in the ICU: a platoon commander who'd been dropped on his head from a chopper.

Two men had come into the restaurant. Americans. Civilians. Rouenna and Polly had finished eating but had ordered more beer. The men had noticed them right away and would glance over frequently while eating. You could tell they were not here to relax, these men, but to talk. They brought their heads together, kept their voices low, and spoke rapidly: an exchange of information more than a chat. They gobbled their steaks and salads like starving men. From their haste and the number of times they glanced over, you might have guessed they were eager to get meal and business over so they could go hit on the girls. Certainly it was no surprise when they got up and dragged their chairs over to Rouenna and Polly's table.

One of the men was tall, well over six feet, the kind of gangly giant that made Vietnamese jaws drop.

"Nurses," he said. And when no one contradicted him: "Told you so, Jeff." Then, as if considering that there might be something presumptuous or even insulting about this snap identification, he oozed a drop of flattery. "Too young to be anything else."

Was it a compliment to be told at twenty-two that you looked young? Here, maybe. Not everyone managed it. (Years from now, descriptions of nurses as well as of soldiers as having *ancient* faces or *ancient* eyes would be commonplace among those looking back at Vietnam.)

The next compliment was just for Polly. "Do you know who Jean Shrimpton is? No? Well, she's a famous model, and you're prettier than her."

The tall man, whose name was Bret, said that he worked for the State Department. He did not say what he did, he did not use the word *classified*, but he made it clear that curiosity about his work could not be satisfied. In fact, he was exactly the type about whose work an army nurse (like the great majority of soldiers) would have had no curiosity at all. He had an apartment in the city and an office at the embassy. But he had been all over South Vietnam, he said. Beautiful country. He spoke Vietnamese to the restaurant's owner and French to the owner's wife. He looked well rested and well fed and strangely pale to eyes that were used to seeing soldiers. He had the kind of clean, cool-and-collected appearance Rouenna had not thought possible in grimy, sticky Vietnam. His shirt looked as white and pressed as if Mamasan had just got done with it. His shoes—tan penny loafers—were scuffless. Beside him Jeff, though neatly dressed too, looked grubby. Jeff was a reporter, and though somewhat older than most of the troops he could have been one of them. His skin was dark, his nose was peeling, and he had something of the same lean-cheeked haggard look of the line dogs. This was true also of the two reporters—one American, one Dutch—who were at this moment among the casualties at the hospital. But it was not true of most. Reporters in general were not popular with the troops, who saw them as belonging to the same system that was using the troops so terribly. Besides, it was common knowledge that the truth about the war was not being delivered to the people back home, and of course the press had to be partly responsible. So there was mistrust and resentment toward reporters—though nothing compared to the hatred of the brass, who would have locked them all up in tiger cages if they could.

If this had been an evening with a normal friend in a normal place and time, Rouenna could have said how things would go

down. The two men would vie for Polly, and the loser would pair
off with Rouenna. There was no bitterness in Rouenna's observation, though she could not help thinking once again how it
would be if *she*— And instantly her thoughts flew back to a different evening, a summer evening many years ago, Palisades
Park, she and her best friend, Beth, and Beth's cousin who was
visiting from California. They were hanging around one of the
most popular rides, hoping to be picked up by boys who would
mistake them, or at least pretend to mistake them, for older than
the fifteen that they were. Hours had been spent on the disguise:
gobbing on makeup, teasing hair, padding bras. Two boys
bopped up, and the cuter one asked the California cousin to go
on the ride. The other boy turned to Beth. Though it was noisy
where they stood and Beth spoke so Rouenna would not hear,
Rouenna understood how Beth replied. So the boy bought three
tickets, and they all three climbed into one of the huge metal
chairs. It was one of those Tilt-a-Whirls on which people are
squeezed and flung against one another, this way then that. For
part of the ride the lights were turned out and the music was
cranked up, the tilting and whirling got much faster and rougher,
and everyone screamed. Sitting in the middle, the boy put an arm
around each girl's shoulders.

The ride could not have lasted more than five minutes, but
by the end of that time Rouenna had made sure that it was Beth
who would be the one left boyless that night.

The men wanted to take Rouenna and Polly to one of the
rooftop nightclubs. Bret tried to cajole them. "Come on, now,
girls, the night is young. And why else did you two put on party
dresses? Surely not so you could spend the night all alone."

The dresses were a gift from *Un*lucky. Sewing was his way of relaxing off duty. ("It's in the blood. All the way back to Palermo we're tailors.") Soon after he arrived, he had ordered a Singer from the Sears and Roebuck catalog and bought bolts of beautiful flowered silk from a Chinese shop in Cholon. Over time he made long loose sleeveless shifts for all the nurses. Some of the nurses didn't really like them because they thought they looked too much like hippie dresses. But the pleasure of peeling off baggy, filthy, bloodstained fatigues and slipping on the cool weightless silk was hard to resist. With the dresses the women wore sandals.

"These aren't party dresses," Polly said. Rouenna could tell that Bret was getting on Polly's nerves. Rouenna took a Kool from her pack, and as Jeff fished a Zippo out of his pocket to light it he said, "Well, you sure look good in them, whatever they are." He said it soothingly, as if he too were worried about Polly's nerves.

Well, if they didn't want to go to a club, would they at least stay for another beer?

"We have to catch our ride back to the base," Polly said, too fast and too firmly for Rouenna to contradict. Besides, it was true. They had only been killing time.

But as they said good-bye, Rouenna felt a twinge. She had briefly allowed herself the fantasy that this really was an evening with a normal friend in a normal place and time, and she had imagined them pairing off, she with the loser, who she fantasized that night would be Jeff. After the nightclub, where they would dance under the stars, he would take her back to his room, at the Hotel Continental. He would pour them drinks and put on some music, and they would dance one last dance, in the dark. She had never gone with a man to a hotel before. She had never been with a reporter. One shrug, and the dress a silk puddle at her feet. Her chance to prove that he had not been the loser after all.

Later, back at their hooch, the women got drunk—drunker— and Polly made fun of Bret, mimicking the way he said "beautiful country" and "the night is still young."

And what about Jeff? Rouenna said. Polly shook her head: not her type.

In the way that can happen when you are drunk, Rouenna opened her mouth to say one thing and something entirely different came out. What came out was the story of what had happened that time at Palisades Park, a story that up till then she had kept to herself.

After a pause, Rouenna asked Polly what she thought, and Polly sighed gustily and said she thought that Rouenna had done enough good deeds in Vietnam to make up for all the sins she had committed in her entire life. Rouenna had never thought about it like this. She had not been to confession since she was a kid, and now she imagined the priest's weary, smoke-roughened voice prescribing not the usual ten Hail Marys or Our Fathers but a year in hell. From the sober look on Polly's face, Rouenna guessed that her friend's thoughts were now turned upon sins of her own. Polly was Catholic, too, of course; not many nurses in Vietnam weren't.

Perhaps Polly also meant to say something entirely different from what now came out of her mouth: "That duck was fucking delicious."

Before she went to sleep that night, thinking of that delicious duck and how it was the best thing she had ever tasted, Rouenna made a vow never to eat duck again. And drunk as she was when she made this vow, she remembered it as soon as she woke up the next morning.

Her first Christmas back in the States, Rouenna received a card from Polly. It was their first communication since they had left each other in Long Binh. With the card Polly enclosed a photograph of her baby son. For several years after that, every Christmas, Rouenna received a card and a photograph of the boy. It was not until the third year that a family resemblance showed. ("I just wish I could *do* something for her, man.")

Some years when the card arrived in the mail, Rouenna would not open it right away. She would lay the envelope aside and wait a day or two or even longer.

Vietnam. The taste of duck, the touch of silk, a soldier reaching across a table with his napkin to dry the tears from a woman's face.

Vietnam. Rouenna had kept her vow. She had never eaten duck again.

It was Gigi barking that returned Rouenna to New Jersey, 1980.

Minutes later, her mother walked into the bedroom and found Rouenna bustling about the closet. "What did you do, Roro, take a nap? Looks like you hardly made any progress at all."

Driving back to Manhattan that night, Rouenna tuned the radio to the oldies station and turned the volume up loud. She often did this when she was in the car alone, and if a song to which she knew the words came on she would sing at the top of her voice. The only kind of music she had ever cared about or wanted to hear now was rock and roll—songs from the late forties to the late seventies—and this particular radio station never played anything else.

After she left Vietnam, the list of things that could take her back was endless: a certain type of weather, a certain shade of green, almost any really bad smell, almost any sudden loud noise, also any ripping sound as of cloth being torn, the waiters at the Hunan Garden (a year among the Vietnamese did not mean she could tell them apart from other Orientals), a certain type of guy, or even just a part of some guy: biceps, tattoo. One winter she would go without heat rather than live with the radiators in the apartment she was renting, which had her waking in the night and straining to tell whether that *purr*-putt, *purr*-putt was the sound of dustoffs just coming into range. Sometimes, especially in the case of loud noises or bad smells, she would feel her pulse accelerating, and for hours afterward or even all day she might be tense or moody. But it was music that affected her most, certain songs flooding her with longings so keen, she wanted to throw back her head and howl.

Rock and roll. In barracks and in bunkers, in every lounge and club, on the hospital wards, in the operating room, in the morgue. As inescapable as the racket of war: *whoosh*, *kaboom*, wah-wah wail. Troops carried transistor radios or portable record or cassette players everywhere, including on operations. ARVN commanders shook their heads: *Enemy always know where GI!* But even the Communists understood: in the prisons of the North, American rock was played as a reward for good behavior, a treat for Christmas and the Fourth of July.

Theme songs. "Ballad of the Green Berets," sacred to many officers, not just Special Forces. (On the same LP, a cut called "Salute to the Nurses.") "We Gotta Get Out of This Place,"

"Eight Miles High," "I Feel Like I'm Fixin' to Die Rag," "Run Through the Jungle"—these were the songs the troopers could not hear often enough. And these were some of the songs that Rouenna had brought home, on a tape that had been made specially for her, a farewell gift presented at the enlisted men's club one night just before she left country.

The tape was her only souvenir. No ashtrays from famous Saigon hot spots, no Ho Chi Minh sandals, no pieces of enemy flags or uniforms. No pieces of enemy. The gewgaws displayed by Vietnamese street peddlers had never tempted her, either. In Hong Kong, on R and R, she had bought a set of bone chinaware, white with gold trim, and had it shipped to the States, intending it for a wedding present for whichever of her two brothers married first. The acoustic guitar she had bought (but never learned to play) she left behind in Long Binh with the GI who turned out to be her DEROS patient.

She got thirty days' leave on her return from overseas, and just about all she did during that time was sleep and listen to her tape. While she was gone, her brother Thad had become a hippie, hair like a blond Indian brave, kept clear of his face with a beaded headband. Like all his tribe, he hated the military and was bummed to have a sister taking part in the war. The whole year she was gone, he had never once written to her. One day he and some friends got stoned, got the munchies, and defrosted the red, white, and blue sheet cake that the Italian baker had made for Rouenna. She would have been angry when her mother wrote to tell her this, except that she knew she was just going to throw the cake out anyway when she got home, so much had her feelings changed. Now that she had come back not only antiwar herself but as big a pothead as he or any of his friends, Thad was happy to forgive her. He was one of his high school's main deal-ers, and a good one, with the best Newark connections. In the morning before he left the house, he would leave Rouenna two or three fat, expertly rolled joints, and she would pass the day alone in her room, smoking and listening to her tape. Not a thing in the world she wanted to do those thirty days back in the U.S.A. but stay high and listen to the Doors, the Byrds, the Beatles, the Stones, the Dead, the Who, Santana, Joplin, and Hendrix.

Who knows how long this might have gone on had not Lieu-tenant Zycinksi had to report for duty. Four months of military service to go. How would she ever survive them?

The hospital at Fort Dix had its share of war wounded, but it was a whole other world from Vietnam. For one thing, no one gave a damn about your having served in the war. You were state-side now, where a colonel's ingrown toenail was worth more fuss than any private's missing feet. Rank, rules, bureaucracy: in Nam, you could forget about this part of army life for at least some of the time. Here you couldn't forget for five minutes before some-one reminded you. ("Get the wrinkles out of that uniform, lieu-tenant." "You didn't fill out the form, lieutenant." "I didn't hear 'sir,' lieutenant.") Four months passed like four years.

But when she finally got her discharge and moved on to jobs at civilian hospitals, things did not much improve. Work in gen-eral had become a problem for Rouenna. She was her father's daughter: she did not like people telling her what to do. "For someone who's been in the army, you sure have a hell of a hard time taking orders," marveled one supervisor.

The lowliness of the nurse's position—something else Rouenna had forgotten about. A position with many (mostly unpleasant) duties but little real responsibility. Never to make her own decisions, never to be trusted not to screw up. Ask a doctor to do this, to do that, even if you've done the procedure yourself many times before. Ask, even if the doctor on duty is only some intern or resident with less experience than you. Ask. Inexperienced, overworked, and frazzled though he may be, he will understand completely that you cannot be trusted. Nod when he troubles to put this into words, and appreciate how he raises his voice so you will be sure to hear him and how he never allows the presence of others, not even patients, to inhibit him.

But to be fair, Rouenna was shocked at how inept many of the nurses she worked with were. Call it self-fulfilling prophecy: they were timid, indecisive, untrustworthy—the opposite of most combat nurses, and by comparison unskilled. Rouenna had been that kind of nurse, too, once upon a time, but it was not a time she cared to remember, and she'd be damned if she was going to be that kind of nurse again. Constant friction. *Who told you to*—she got so sick of hearing those words. (Words. This too she had forgotten: stateside, *fuck* and *shit* meant something else. Oh, the things that got people upset here back in the world! *Motherfucker:* say it and lose your job.)

Rouenna was shocked as well at how inefficiently stateside hospital wards were run compared with those in Vietnam. Not that her opinions or suggestions were appreciated. No one was interested in what she might have learned as a combat nurse, none of the other nurses she worked with were curious about her wartime experiences, and like most people they never asked her anything about Vietnam.

Equally disturbing to Rouenna was the behavior of the one nurse she met who was also a veteran of the Army Nurse Corps, an older woman, maybe thirty, called Willa, who'd been at Qui Nhon a few years before Rouenna's own tour began. Rouenna would not even have known about Willa's military service had it not been for one of the patients, a veteran who was suffering from multiple health problems and who refused to be treated at the VA hospital. This veteran, an ex-rifleman named Chuck, knew about Willa only because their families were acquainted. She never spoke to him about the war. And she was not exactly hostile to Rouenna, but she avoided her. Willa was quiet and shy-seeming around most people, kept to herself, never had much to say. Changed the subject when Chuck or Rouenna brought up Vietnam. The two women worked together just fine—at least Willa knew what she was doing—but it was clear that there could never be the kind of camaraderie that would have arisen naturally between them in Vietnam. Honestly no big deal, since Rouenna herself tended more and more not to want to talk about the war. What bothered her, though, was the awkwardness between them. This woman did not want to meet her eye. Rouenna thought of a time when her father was dying and she and her mother had gone to the hospital to see him. He was in his final throes then, never to regain consciousness, and when they entered his room they found him sprawled on his back, his hospital gown bunched under his chin, the bedcovers bunched at his feet. His legs were wide apart, his penis was pointing head-ward—it looked like a hard-on. He was a shocking sight, and after Rouenna's mother dashed forward to cover him they both stood there speechless, unable to look each other in the eye.

Either of them would have given a year of her life to undo the preceding minute. Rouenna would remember it always, more vividly than the actual moment of death.

But what was it between her and Willa that kept bringing back that particular obscene memory? It wearied Rouenna, trying to make sense of it, and she was relieved when she quit that job and did not have to deal with Willa anymore.

She didn't miss nursing at all. It was not just dirty, thankless, frustrating work. It was boring. Most of what took place in a hospital, even in the emergency room, was routine, and Rouenna knew that the challenges she had faced daily in Nam were not to be found anywhere stateside except on TV. Not much excitement, not much opportunity for a nurse to feel heroic, Superwomanish, *valuable*. Rouenna remembered how apathetically she had chosen nursing in the first place, how low her expectations of that career had been (like many other women, she had thought of nursing as something to do only until she got married and started a family), how she had never liked either the training or the work, and how all that changed completely when she got to Danang.

But in the end it was not the boring routine or the condescending doctors or the constant clashes with authority but the patients themselves who were probably most responsible for driving Rouenna from nursing. The dressing was too tight, the Foley itched, the pills were too big to swallow. How could they be expected to eat this food. What did she mean, they couldn't eat anything for eight hours. Why hadn't she come on the first ring. This medicine was making them fart. How many times did they have to have blood taken, didn't she know that it hurt. Needles scared them, X-rays scared them, surgery was the end of the world. *Don't be such a wimp,* she snapped at a lawyer with kidney stones. And of course he complained and of course she got chewed out for it.

"You can't expect ordinary civilians to behave like marines," the head nurse told her.

An image of one of those eighteen-year-old marines came back to her.

"You know that kidney stones can be very painful."

Both eyes, both arms, both legs.

Ordinary civilians. As if Rouenna hadn't seen plenty of those in the evacuation hospitals, too. Still saw them—in fact, it was the strangest thing. Home now for more than a year, dealing every day with patients who behaved like small children, Rouenna kept seeing those other children, from the war. She was old enough to remember the thalidomide crisis and how horrified the world had been when those several thousand children were born deformed. But the war was deforming children every day—Rouenna had no idea what the actual figure was, but she knew it had to be many times higher than several thousand. And at least no one had planted thalidomide in those women's wombs, unlike the booby traps and land mines that were often planted where everyone knew children were going to be. And of course you could never remember those wounded children without remembering what every American witness found so hard to believe: how quietly they bore their pain.

Well, if those kids wouldn't scream, by god Rouenna would. *In Nam I treated a six-year-old girl covered with napalm burns who made less of a fuss than you!*

She was not a bad woman, the head nurse. "Look, hon," she said. "You're home now. You've got to adjust. For your own good." She was right. And kidney stones were excruciating, right up there with childbirth, and Rouenna did know that. She was turning into a monster. And why couldn't she control herself? (At the time, she was living with her mother, who had a neighbor who often dropped by. This woman had a lesion on her hand that was surely malignant. Every time Rouenna saw her, she urged her to go to the doctor. But the woman was too scared. Dutifully Rouenna kept after her until one day the woman exploded. "Stop trying to talk me into letting some stranger cut my hand!" A rage she had hardly known was in her had Rouenna lashing back. "Okay, so die then!" Monstrous.)

But say Rouenna was completely in the wrong—was it too much to expect at least a smidgen of shame from some of these patients?

Never happen.

"That's what you get for going over there where you had no business being."

Rouenna surprised herself. Instead of throttling the man as she would have expected herself to do, she went to pieces. It was as if someone had twisted a knife in her, she could not believe how much it hurt—and *now* who was the wimp who could not take pain?

Where you had no business being.

She could remember men so badly hurt they could barely breathe forcing themselves to speak. *Thank you, nurse. God bless you, lieutenant. You are so beautiful.* How brave they were, and how brave she felt among them—that was how they made all the nurses feel, brave and beautiful. Was she ever going to feel that way again?

She knew where she wanted to be, all right. So: should she reenlist?

Her lover, Chuck, the vet she had met in the hospital, put it to her straight. "You would have to be crazy." It didn't take much thinking for Rouenna to see it this way, too. Had it been earlier in the war, it might have been different. But she knew how things were going over there, with so-called Vietnamization, and more and more American troops being withdrawn, and the morale of those left behind at an all-time low. There was still fighting, of course, and there were still casualties, but Rouenna knew that many of the patients she'd be treating this time around would be addicts and psych cases. And even if this hadn't been so, when she looked at it honestly, she knew she wasn't capable of going through another tour. She had had enough. Even Chuck was turning out to be a little more Vietnam than she could handle. She liked being with him, they had fun together, they understood each other as only two people who'd been through the war could, but she knew she could not attach herself permanently to this permanent casualty. She'd had enough of war, nursing, and casualties.

She had promised herself that when she got back to the world she would do something about her drinking and her cigarette- and pot-smoking, at least cut down if she couldn't give them up, but she did nothing of the kind, and in fact it would be years before she took even the first step.

Many Vietnam returnees were taking advantage of the GI Bill to go back to school, but Rouenna couldn't see herself doing this. No reason to think she'd like school any better than she ever had, and she couldn't see herself fitting in with all those kids.

Her brother was one thing, but to be surrounded by hippie types, half of them trooping around in army jackets—she didn't know if it was true, but she'd heard that those jackets and other pieces of uniforms that were all the rage had been recycled off the bodies of dead grunts. She couldn't see her brother's girlfriend in *her* tattered field jacket (found in a boutique on Manhattan's Eighth Street) without wanting to rip it off.

Control, control, control. Rouenna was working on it, but it wasn't always easy. A campus was probably one of the worst places for her to be right now. Though she didn't have any problem not bringing up the war, she didn't want to be in a position of always having to hide the fact that she had been *where she had no business being.* Her mother was against her going to school, too. "You've already wasted enough time in the army." That time would have been better spent finding a husband, was what she meant. Most of Rouenna's high school friends were married now, and she didn't fit in with them, either. Oh, she knew that she too would be married one day, but right now she didn't want to think about it. She couldn't think about marriage without thinking about children, and when she thought about children she thought about some of the things she was hearing from Chuck. Not that there was any reason to panic. In fact, so far there was no scientific evidence at all for Chuck's suspicions. But he and some other veterans had begun to believe that the cause of the many ailments afflicting them—rashes, headaches, tumors, asthma, joint pain—was the herbicides to which they had been exposed while serving in Vietnam. There was even some talk of a possible link to cancer and to malformations and diseases in veterans' children. Rouenna had no idea how serious the risk of birth defects actually was (from all she could tell, Pretty Polly's baby was normal), but she didn't think it was a bad idea to wait until more information came to light. Again, she remembered thalidomide. She had been a kid when she saw those photographs, and they had haunted her into adulthood as she was sure they had haunted every kid who saw them. And of course she remembered the eyeless baby. God. Wasn't that all she needed.

She wasn't confused. She knew what she wanted. She wanted a job. She wanted enough money to support herself. She wanted to find her own apartment and move out of her mother's place. New York City: millions of jobs and apartments. She could be near her family and a whole world away from them at the same time—that was the beauty of New York. Once she had accepted the idea that no work was ever going to measure up to the highs of combat nursing, she didn't really much care what kind of work she found. Again: she was her father's daughter. *A job was a job and one was just like another . . .* And besides, she was still planning on marriage and children.

Over the years she would end up doing a lot of waitressing, and spring 1980 found her in the middle of one of her best gigs, a midtown steakhouse serving mostly businessmen (some seatings you would not see a single female at any table), where the hardest thing she had to remember was medium or rare, and the tips were expense-account generous. The owner was generous, too, treating his girls every payday to the full works: twelve-ounce sirloins, onion rings, hash browns, creamed spinach, and pineapple cheesecake.

The year before, one of the other waitresses had got married and moved out of town, and Rouenna was able to get the lease on the woman's apartment. It was the kind of apartment that was becoming almost impossible to find in Manhattan: rent stabilized, big enough for a couple, in a safe, clean, quiet building on Thirty-second Street, near Third Avenue. Having moved over the past several years from one unsatisfactory place to another, Rouenna had begun to believe that living in Manhattan was a dream she was going to have to give up. So she could not have been happier with this stroke of luck—she wasn't used to being lucky. (More than likely, though, she would have been jolted right out of that happiness had anyone been able to tell her that she would be in that same apartment—uncoupled—for the next dozen years.)

The radio station she was tuned to wasn't playing songs Rouenna associated with her tour—the disc jockey was into an earlier era. "Will You Still Love Me Tomorrow," "Walk Like a Man," "He's So Fine," "Up on the Roof," "Dancing in the Street," "Louie, Louie," "Don't Worry, Baby," "Twist and Shout." Now, these were all fine songs, too, and good to hear. The high school gym decorated with balloons and crepe-paper streamers. Girls with stiff hair, in chiffon dresses with matching high heels—heels that had to be kicked off for the fast dances.

"Only Love Can Break a Heart." "And Then He Kissed Me." She knew all the words. She sang along.

She did not think it was an exaggeration to say that, without her little Sony player, she would not have survived the war. Sometimes when she could not get to sleep, either because she was too upset or because the Dexedrine she had taken had not worn off, she would comfort herself by just resting and listening to music, until it was time to get up, pop more Dexedrine, and go back to work.

"Follow the Boys." This deejay knew she was out there.

For a long time after she came home—long past her month's leave—Rouenna would listen to the tape the men had made for her at least once a day. But then it got to be more like once a week, once a month, once in a while—she would have to be in a certain mood to want to hear it, a mood that happened less and less. Inevitably came a period when you could not have got Rouenna to play that tape for anything. She got over that, but still for long stretches she would forget that she even had the tape. One day when she hadn't listened to it for what seemed to her must have been years, she had a great yearning to hear it, and when she dug it out and put it on she discovered that it was damaged. She could still hear some of the music, but it was distorted now by a strange metallic chirping, like some alien birdsong. Even so, it brought her back. The Quonset ward with its long double row of beds. The radio tuned to AFVN. Patsy Cline. The volume up loud enough so that the women washing the floors had to raise their voices to carry on their chatter. The infantry sergeant half out of his mind with phantom pain propping himself up on one elbow to scream, "Will somebody get these fucking gook cunts to shut the fuck up! This is a great fucking song, man! And I wanna fucking hear it!"

Rouenna had managed to quiet the women then—but what could she do now? As the tape continued to play, the problem only got worse, the music harder and harder to hear, until it was all but obliterated by the chirping.

She didn't throw the tape away. She kept it, even though she knew she would never be able to listen to it again, just as she kept the silk dress *Un*lucky had made for her years after she no longer fit into it, not even close, not even at her thinnest, no, no, never again. And then one day both tape and dress disappeared. Meaning, though she didn't remember doing so, she must have thrown them away, probably when she was moving from one apartment to another. The fact simply struck her one morning when she was on her way to work, that these two things were no longer among her possessions. But that is what happens to possessions as the years roll by, if you are not careful, if you are not sentimental. The only mementos of Nam she had left were a couple of snapshots. She knew where they were, but when was the last time she had looked at them? Come to think of it, what had happened to her uniforms, her lieutenants' bars, her Army Commendation Medal, her Bronze Star?

She had driven far enough now that she was beginning to lose the station she was tuned to. She was getting a little static and drift. She was just about to turn the dial when the disc jockey announced the next solid-gold hit: "It's Shelley Fabares, it's 1962, and the song is 'Johnny Angel.'"

Part THREE

As often happens in this part of the country, there is a snowstorm in the middle of spring. And though it happens often, it never fails to take people by surprise—how could it not be a surprise to wake up to cherry trees hung with bloom *and* snow. There is snow inside each tulip and daffodil. Walking across campus, I see a cardinal pulsing on a bough halfway up a snow-covered fir, like the heart of the fir. Then I catch sight of his mate. (*What happened to Romeo and Juliet?*)

A student who has an appointment with me is waiting outside my office. When I let her in, she sees the books piled on my desk and says, "Oh, Vietnam." Immediately she adds, "I've been to the Wall." (Hers is the generation that at the word *Vietnam* will always immediately think *the Wall*.) "I cried," she says. Wistful.

An hour later, on her way out, she casts another (dubious, wistful) glance at the books and says, "Good luck. I can't even watch those movies."

Among the books on my desk are two by a writer I have known for years, a man who was a foot soldier in Vietnam in 1966 and 1967 and who also teaches college now, in Philadelphia. He has written one novel and one memoir about the war. He has been back to Vietnam four times. Although he made those four trips partly to do research for his books, he has told me that he would have gone back anyway and that he intends to keep going back as often as he can. It's like a spell, he says. His books do not earn much money, but every penny earned so far has gone to the Vietnam Red Cross. Recently, he has begun writing poems about Vietnam. I don't think he has ever written about anything but Vietnam, and it is a good if idle question what he would have been writing about all these years, if writing at all, had he stayed home.

I remember talking to Rouenna about this man and about all the other veterans who had been back, and about those other Americans who were not veterans but who had visited and revisited Vietnam. I wanted to know, of course, whether she would ever consider making such a trip herself. I had trouble believing she had no desire at all to visit Vietnam in peacetime. I had to remind myself that she never went anywhere. She did not travel, she did not take vacations, she had never visited any place as a tourist in her life. Whatever had lured her into joining the army, it was not, as it was for a sad number of others, that lie about seeing the world. Though Ho Chi Minh City is high on the list of places I myself would like to go, I never told Rouenna this. Something always stopped me from saying it.

My friend—the writer, the veteran—was not particularly interested in Rouenna's story. He had never been wounded, and though he knew there were nurses in-country he had never met one. He did not see them as having had much of a role in the great Vietnam epic. A footnote, he said. Whenever we were together and I started talking about Rouenna, he would stare off.

In another memoir, by another writer, a hospitalized GI complains that the army nurses aren't pretty enough. Should be a job prerequisite, this GI says. The patient in the next bed asks, "Now, why would a beautiful girl join the army?" To which another patient, who is black, responds, "Now, why would anyone look twice at a white chick here in a land of Oriental good and plenty?" There follows a raucous argument up and down the ward.

Rouenna: "Yeah, it could make you jealous, the way some of the guys talked about the Vietnamese girls. Me, I thought they were exaggerating, I didn't think those girls were so gorgeous. Except this one I saw who was all dressed up—it was her wedding day—and she was really something, she was like a perfect little China doll. I think what a lot of guys liked about these girls was how doll-like and delicate they were. You could pick them up with one hand. But everyone knew most guys would have chosen a plain blond round-eye over the most beautiful girl in Vietnam. The white guys would, anyway. Besides, the guys who had Vietnamese girlfriends, a lot of them didn't treat those girls too well. Sometimes you got the feeling that what some guys liked about having Vietnamese girls was that you could do whatever you wanted to them. It was like having an Oriental slave."

(A diner on Lexington Avenue, midtown, sometime in the early seventies. A couple sitting in the booth behind mine. The man does not bother to lower his voice. "I told you, girl. Don't you ever, ever step in front of me again. *You walk three paces behind me at all times.* You forget again, and I'll break every bone in your body and ship the pieces back to the hole where I found you, *chop-chop.*" Though I have not eaten yet, I get up and walk out. From the sidewalk I look through the plate-glass window and see the woman sitting silently with bowed head.)

"There were always a couple of battered women on the Vietnamese wards—battered kids, too. The kids who had it the worst were the ones that were half American. Maybe worst of all were the ones that were half black. Most of these kids didn't belong to anyone, they lived in the street." What the Vietnamese called "life's dust."

More footnotes: Among the small number of American women killed in Vietnam were some who were shot or stabbed by GIs.

By 1972, on some campuses, on my campus, the women's liberation movement had grown bigger than the antiwar movement. A speaker at a rally told the crowd, "If you want to know why things like My Lai happen, just go out there and pick ten men at random and ask them whether they have ever in their lives tortured or killed a helpless animal just for fun."

I knew this was rhetoric. I didn't have to do as the speaker said to get the point she was trying to make. But curiosity got the better of me.

"It was just a turtle."

"Do bullfrogs count?"

"Of course. I'm a hunter."

"See, my brother caught this mouse . . ."

"Is it okay if I don't answer?"

I quit before I reached ten.

Once back in the States, Rouenna said, she stopped paying attention to what was happening in Vietnam. She did not read the papers or watch the news. All she really knew was that the war was coming to an end. During the last days of Saigon, she happened to catch a special program on TV. About a dozen men were seated on a stage in front of a small audience, talking and answering questions. All the men had been in the war, either as soldiers or as reporters. The reporters talked about the Gulf of Tonkin incident, the turning point of the Tet offensive, Vietnamization, the Cambodian incursion, the Paris peace talks—things about which Rouenna's understanding was and would always be hazy. The veterans talked about how hard it was to come home, how they were treated like criminals, how no one wanted to hear what had happened to them, and how even those who'd been against the war themselves were still mad as hell at the peaceniks and draft dodgers and Jane Fonda. It was the first time Rouenna had heard these things spoken out loud. Watching the program, she learned many facts she had not known. Figures: how many Americans had served, how many had been killed, how many Vietnamese on both sides were believed to have been killed. (The number of Americans killed was lower and the number of Vietnamese killed much higher than Rouenna would have guessed.) She wasn't sure she wanted to go on watching—she had turned on the television to watch *Kojak*—but what kept her from changing the channel was those vets: not what they were saying but the way they looked. Had it been that long? No. They had aged overnight. They had let themselves go. She was thinking, of course, of the fit young men she had known. These paunchy guys could have been those boys' fathers. And yet the oldest could not have been over thirty.

It was not a program about veterans, it was a play about veterans. These were actors who had never been in Vietnam. The illusion was fleeting, but the sense of unreality stayed with Rouenna, so hard was it for her to make the connection between the men she was watching and those soldiers of just a few years ago. And there was the way they were dressed. Jungle fatigues, rock T-shirts, bandanna headbands or scarves—one guy was wearing his boonie hat. Some, including one sitting in a wheelchair in the front row, had on dark or mirrored sunglasses. They all had what Rouenna thought of as The Look. Chuck had it, and so did other veterans she had since met. If this really had been a play, this was just what the costume designer would have come up with. It was a raggedy-ass look; out from under that boonie hat escaped tufts of wild hair. A scraggly, scruffy, raggedy-ass look, but it didn't just happen, just as it didn't just happen that the reporters were all wearing jackets and ties. *I was there* said The Look. Some vets would keep it unchanging for years, and for years men of all ages who had never been there would dress up just like them, war wannabes.

From their questions it was clear that people in the audience were less interested in what had happened to the men while they were in Vietnam than in what happened to them after they came home. One after another the men spoke of the hostility with which they'd been treated by fellow Americans—some said they even feared for their lives.

"I felt safer in the jungle, man!" the vet in the wheelchair shouted.

But when the time came for her to be asked this same question (and that time was not far away), Rouenna would say that the response she remembered was not so much hostility as boredom. Her mother was a good example: "Whenever I'd start talking about Vietnam, her eyelids would droop." As for people not wanting to hear about the work she did in the war, well, it was certainly true that they did not want to hear about it. But she was a nurse. She was used to that—nurses and doctors did not expect other people to want to hear about what they did all day long. "You don't talk about gangrene over dinner."

It was not long after Rouenna saw the TV program that the requests began to come.

For a book about the role of women in the Vietnam War, we would like to hear from any woman, military or civilian, who was there.

For an oral history project, we would like to interview women who served in any branch of the military during the Vietnam War.

For a study about American nurses in Vietnam, we would appreciate your help in completing the enclosed questionnaire.

If you would like to share your experiences as a Vietnam War veteran, please contact us at . . .

For a collection of memoirs . . .

For a collection of letters . . .

If you would like to contribute any photographs . . .

As the song goes, It's been a long time coming. But the time to tell your personal story is finally here.

Please answer the following questions concerning any health problems you may have experienced since your return from overseas.

It happened for years: "I'd be out somewhere, in the street, say, or riding the train, and I'd see some guy at a distance, and my

heart would stop." In every single case it was a mistake. A ludi-
crous mistake, "because the guy I'd be looking at would be
some kid, nineteen, twenty, but in reality it was five, ten, fifteen
years later." And what she felt then, Rouenna said, "was like
some dirty low-down trick had been played on me." With time
the trick happened less and less, but the pain—the pain was
never less. "You see, during the war, everyone rotated in and out
on a different date, so you had people coming and going all the
time, and you were never sure what happened to them after you
last saw them. With the patients, we only had them at most a
couple of days. Then the ones who recovered went back to fighting the war, and the rest were evacuated to hospitals in Japan or
back in the States, and you never knew which guys made it and
which guys didn't, though in some cases you could make a good
guess. Anyway, you'd put those guys out of your mind and get
on with the next batch. But there were some you'd always be
wondering about. Like that marine sergeant I told you about,
from the Island. Like what's he doing now? How did his wife
react to no hands? And those two that got engaged in Long
Binh. Did he survive his tour in one piece, and are they married
now? Do they have kids, and do those kids have any birth
defects?"

Even if she'd wanted to, she could not have learned what
happened to this or that person because she did not remember
names.

"I knew nurses who made a habit of never reading the name
tags of the guys that came in hit. In nursing school they try to tell
you how important it is to be personal, you know: always address
the patient by name. But believe me, in a situation of mass casualties, that little personal touch could be fatal."

In fact, she never made any attempt to communicate with anyone she had known in Vietnam. "I didn't even respond to Polly's
Christmas cards. Which I guess is why she stopped sending them."

Living in Manhattan, she could easily have joined in the celebra-
tions and reunions that took place, first in 1982, at the dedication
of the Vietnam Veterans Memorial in Washington, D.C., or three
years later, at the dedication of the New York Vietnam Veterans
Memorial and welcome-home parade. Many women veterans
did. "I didn't have any problem with other people doing their
thing, but me, I couldn't get into it." Again, she caught some
coverage of these events in newspapers and magazines and on
TV. And again she experienced the same sense of unreality that
she had experienced that time in 1975 (and that she would
always experience to some degree or other when confronted
with any retrospection or revisiting of the war).

She had never been to the Wall. She would make it down to
Washington one of these days, she said, but no hurry. "I mean,
that's the point about it being a memorial, right? It will always
be there."

Maybe the prospect was just too daunting. To be faced with
all those names. Not to be able to recall a single one.

But maybe visiting the memorial would have changed her
feeling that it was "just a wall." What she actually said was, "There
was what I saw with my own eyes and what I touched with my
own hands, and now there's this"—groping blindly before throwing up her hands. "It's just a wall."

More and more she came to understand Willa, the nurse whose
behavior had mystified her that first year home from the war.

Once, Rouenna overheard someone she worked with talking about her on the phone—"She's okay. Very quiet. No, not unfriendly, just shy"—and she didn't mind hearing herself described that way. In fact she was not shy, she was not very quiet, but she didn't mind keeping people at a distance and her feelings to herself. She was not in the habit of talking about herself, and people who did talk a lot, about themselves and about what they were feeling, these were not Rouenna's favorite people. It always bothered her when she heard her mother or someone else say "I had a good cry." And if she heard someone talk about how much they had cried, at a movie, say, or at the Wall, or at the death of someone they didn't know—Princess Di, Jackie O—she knew she was probably not going to get along with that person. That was the kind of person Rouenna did not trust. She believed that it came naturally to people who talked a lot about themselves to lie. In some cases the person might think that what he or she was saying was true, but mostly (Rouenna believed) people knew perfectly well that they were lying and, even when they were talking about their own feelings, would tell you what they thought you wanted to hear. Put another way? She thought most people were full of shit.

Often when she heard someone telling a story about Vietnam, she knew that most likely it had not happened exactly the way it was being told. One night when she and Chuck had first got together, they went out drinking with an old high school friend of Chuck's and the friend's date. The friend told a very long story about Vietnam—he'd only just come back. Later, when she and Chuck were alone, Rouenna said what she had refrained from saying in front of the girl that ex-GI had been trying so hard to impress: That story was a load of waterbullshit (her word for less-than-true stories about Vietnam) and you know it. "Chuck just shrugged and said, 'What difference does it make? It was a great story.' He didn't have any problem with it. But I did. I sure did." So much so that, though I pressed her, she would not repeat the story. "I told you, it wasn't true."

Vietnam made me do it. Now, here was something Rouenna could really get worked up about. "Guys using the war as an excuse for fucking up every which way later on." (She would have appreciated a story written by one of my students, about a vet whose first act upon coming home was to walk out on his wife and the daughter who'd been born while he was at war. This is a true story, the student told the class. Not till she was in high school did her father finally explain himself, in a letter declaring that what had happened to him in Vietnam made it impossible for him to fulfill his family obligations when he returned. She never wrote back to him, but in her story she demands to know why what had happened to him in Vietnam had not made it also impossible for him to find a new wife and start a new family when he returned. She called the story "PTSD," explaining that the title was meant to be ironic—because of course it was her own trauma and victimhood that the story went on to explore. Entered in the school's annual fiction competition, "PTSD" took first prize.)

And now it is I who am groping, but before I throw up *my* hands, let me try to get this thought down. I believe that at times Rouenna was troubled by the same fear that I have seen expressed by a certain writer, the fear that the more stories that got told, the more novels and memoirs and movies and TV shows about the Big Event that got put out into the world, the greater the gap between those imagined or reconstructed versions and the Big Event itself. Only the Big Event the writer was talking about was the Holocaust, and the writer was Primo Levi.

I should have known she would not like the movie *The English Patient*. We'd been talking about movies that have nurses as main characters (there are very few), and when she said she had never seen *The English Patient* I suggested she rent it. It was the first movie she had rented in a long while. She hardly ever went to movie theaters anymore. If she wanted to see a new movie, she usually decided to wait until it came out on video, but by that time more often than not she would have lost interest. So it had happened with *The English Patient*. (And this was yet another way in which she was completely different from me and my other friends, who see everything. Immediately.)

She was surprised that I had missed something so obvious: it would have been impossible for that one nurse to care for her severely burned patient all by herself. "How on earth did she turn him? She wouldn't have had to give him morphine at the end, she would have killed him long before." It annoyed her that the author had not got this right. (I didn't dare say what difference does it make, it was a great story.) As for the nurse smilingly sharing a plum with her patient, or falling asleep almost on top of him in the same bed, Rouenna could not see her doing that. "Not with a crispy critter." Rouenna herself had automatically covered her mouth and nose with her palm during certain scenes. And still she could smell it. She could smell it even after the movie had ended and she had turned the set off. All that night, she said, her apartment reeked of it.

She was disappointed that I had not picked up on these little inauthenticities. She made me feel dumb and ashamed. But I don't remember anyone else picking up on them, either. Perhaps everyone was too busy having a good cry.

I knew that, like the English patient's nurse, Rouenna had been an Angel of Death. It is this that I have the most difficulty imagining. Slipping behind the curtain during a lull to check on the expectants, finding one who is conscious ("I'm in a world of hurt here, lieutenant, can you help me?"), preparing the morphine injection ("You'll be out of that hurt real soon now, I promise"), wiping the mud and blood from his face, pressing her cheek to his cheek, silently saying good-bye. Later, there'd be the letter to write to his parents.

Now, when I try to imagine this, I suppose it is not really surprising that the scene presents itself to me like a scene from a movie. Two larger-than-life faces coming together. To think they would have been about the same age as my undergraduates. One kid helping another kid to die.

Whatever she thought of the movie *The English Patient*, I know she would have agreed with these lines from the book: "Every damn general should have had my job. Every damn general." This is the nurse Hana speaking.

And this is Rouenna:

"What really pissed me off was when we got orders to tidy up the wards, get the men cleaned and shaved, and hide the worst-looking cases, because some fucking general was paying an inspection visit. And I just wanted to grab that general by the scruff of the neck, drag him over to the stinkiest, pussiest, most maggoty wound in the whole fucking place and *rub his nose in it.*"

She would have been a hero to many if she had done that.

I could have guessed that she did not vote. She had never voted. She had no interest in politics at all. But one thing she did believe in was universal conscription—and for her that meant both sexes. She said, "You have to understand: kids died over there because there was a shortage of nurses. Now, if you can draft people and train them to fight, you can draft them and train them to do other things in a war, like nursing. We should not have been working around the clock like that—it was inhuman and it was unfair to the guys. Didn't have enough doctors, either, and in some cases there was even a shortage of supplies. And men died because of that. And to this day I don't understand how Americans could have let it happen. I hated the army and all its lies, but you almost can't blame them for lying to those women. One way or another they had to get more nurses over to Nam. I say they should have been able to draft them."

When I tried to explain that for some women—like me, for example—it would have been impossible, *impossible*, she would not listen. "I'm not saying it was easy, but you never know what you can do till you're forced to do it. Think of the soldiers. They weren't all born to kill, I don't care what they wrote on their helmets." Unconvinced, I said, "I would have been like Polly." "Nah, you're not that pretty." "That is not what I meant."

When Rouenna's brother crashed his motorcycle, her mother said, Thank god I still have one son left. But that son moved away. Henry got married and moved to his wife's hometown of New

Orleans. Rouenna gave him the set of white bone chinaware with gold trim that she had bought in Hong Kong. After he moved, they didn't see much of each other. In the way it sometimes happens, Henry embraced his wife's people and came to think of them as his first family, the ones he should be with on holidays, and so on. His mother was hurt by this, but Rouenna took it in stride. Why pretend the Zycinskis had ever been a close-knit, loving family? In Vietnam she had not tried to hide from the fact that she didn't miss home the way some others did. She wrote only a few letters, and they were always brief and "just to say I'm okay." If she needed and asked for something (tampons, say), her mother would dutifully send it, but Rouenna never expected the fat envelopes and care packages other nurses and soldiers received every mail call. This was the sort of thing your buddies paid attention to, though, and so you were never really left out.

Another death: the woman who lived next door to Rouenna's mother. You were right, you were right, Rouenna's mother said, the resentment in her tone unmistakable. As if being right made Rouenna also somehow responsible.

When I can stand it no longer, I call Rouenna's mother to ask her what happened to Rouenna's parakeets.

"I let them go."

"Go—?"

"In Brooklyn. When we went to clean out the apartment. I let them fly out the window."

"But it was winter."

"Oh, they'll be all right. Animals know how to survive. Did you get the photographs?"

I thank her for the photographs and quickly hang up. I am shaken—and not just because of Romeo and Juliet. It is hard for me to hear that woman's voice. It is Rouenna's voice. And I am afraid of people who beat their children.

The next time I go to the shop where I buy cat food and where birds and small animals also are sold, I ask the manager whether Romeo and Juliet could have survived.

For a little while, maybe, he says. "But not through a bad winter."

Murderer.

Thank god I still have one son left.

Soul murderer.

*

Dog days in the city. Gray, sticky dawn. Unbreathable air. A sky like phlegm. Columbus Circle. Waiting to board the charter bus that goes upstate to the correctional facility where I visit my old friend Luther. I recognize some of the other passengers, women and children. I know the etiquette—never ask what a prisoner is in for or for how long—though it hardly matters since no one ever speaks to me. At most, a nod. This morning an offer of a doughnut from a teenage girl. "My eyes were bigger than my stomach," she says, and she and everyone within hearing giggles: she is hugely pregnant.

The bus driver today is the friendly one (there is another who cracks his contempt over our heads like a whip). As we roll along, he will carry on long conversations with the passengers sitting up front. He is not supposed to, it is against the rules for him to talk while driving, but if he didn't, he says, the job would be too boresome.

Boresome, too boresome, is a good way to describe that ten-hour round-trip ride. I am one of the few making it alone. The bus is full, every seat taken, and we have jammed the overhead racks with bags and packages for the inmates. These will be taken away from us for inspection as soon as we arrive, not to be delivered to the inmates till well after we are gone again. On the bus I have heard high-pitched bitching about packages never delivered to inmates at all, and about the searches to which we must all submit before being allowed to enter the visiting room. Now and then, for reasons never given, a visitor will be singled out and informed that she cannot enter the visiting room unless she agrees to a strip search. I was surprised to discover that almost all the correction officers are white, the tension between them and visitors a good measure of what it must be like between them and inmates. You don't just show up to see someone, of course; the authorities have to know you are coming, your name must appear on your inmate's authorized visitor list. Sometimes there is a mistake, somehow a visitor's name does not appear on the list, whose fault unclear, and if the person doing lobby duty that day is one of those screws with a heart of stone, no amount of pleas or tears will get you past that first locked gate. And sometimes a visitor whose name does appear on the list may find the visit canceled because of some misbehavior on the part of the inmate in the last day or so.

Imagine, then, the anxiety that rides with us on the bus. You never know what might happen when you finally get up there, whether yours will be the name left off the list this time, whether you'll be the one fingered for strip search. Today, with the temperature already in the eighties at dawn, the air conditioner is barely working, blowing just enough air to keep us alive. Soon it is so hot I worry that the bus driver, who is dripping like a marathoner, will pass out and crash. I worry about some of the older women—plenty of grandmothers aboard. I worry about the pregnant girl and about the children—is that one with tongue lolling and eyes rolling back in his head really just asleep? But mostly I worry about myself. *What am I doing here?*

We don't need a thermometer to know that we are well into the nineties. Everyone, even our usually talkative driver, is silent. Earlier a baby spat up, and though his mother wiped the mess the smell remains, growing stronger every mile. It will sit in my nostrils for days. I promise myself that I will never, ever make this trip again.

The driver calls out encouragement. Just hang on a little longer, relief is in sight. He means the twenty-minute rest stop that we always take, and thinking about it—the McDonald's as cold as a meat locker, one giant-sized Coca-Cola with crushed ice coming up—really does help. I remember Rouenna telling me about all those people who said that McDonald's was the first place they wanted to go when they got back from Vietnam, and when the giant yellow M finally appears it's like a glimpse of heaven.

CLOSED TODAY DUE TO BROKEN VENTILATOR.

Like a panicked herd, we round on our driver and demand that he take us straight to some other restaurant. But he is firm. You know I can't do that, he says. Bus can't just drive off the highway like that. Got to wait for the next rest stop.

How far is that? the pregnant girl asks tremulously, and when she hears she whimpers.

Defeatedly we reboard the bus (if it had been the other driver, the one who always treats us with contempt, I am sure we would have pounced and torn him to pieces) and drop into our seats, those upholstered seats into which so much of us has already soaked deep. Our desperation has communicated itself to the children, who are almost all screaming. Some mothers soothe, others snap. *Shut the fuck up!* The bus fills with the noise of smacking and wailing. I am digging my fingers into my ears when someone—one of the grandmothers, sitting way in the back, the hottest part of the bus—starts to sing. It is a song that everyone knows, and after a few bars voices join in. I know it too, it is a song we used to sing in grade school, but I cannot get any sound past the block in my throat, mouthing words the best I can do. Most of the kids have stopped crying to listen, and the ones who know the words are singing along, too. We go through all the verses and it takes a long time. The whole wide world, the wind and the rain, the sun and the moon, the little bitty baby, you and me, brother, you and me, sister, and a-everybody heah-a. In His hands.

The prison isn't air-conditioned, either, but large (carefully guarded) fans are going full blast in the visiting room.

"Luther, you owe me."

"Hey, one day I'll be out of here."

Sometimes I would rather not be reminded of this. If I thought seeing him on the *in*side was complicated . . .

But I bring up my friend Luther at this point for a reason. Partly because of the way he got in touch with me—his mother heard about my first book and sent it to him, he read it and wrote me a letter—he is forever linked in my mind with Rouenna Zycinski. And he is another person I always thought I might write about one day. For a while I even thought I would marry them, Luther and Rouenna, in a story that I had begun to think of as "my Staten Island story."

Though I have mentioned Rouenna to Luther before, this is the first time I tell him how she died and how before she died she asked me to help her write about Vietnam. Luther is not particularly interested in Rouenna, but Vietnam is a thorny issue for him. He might have ended up going there himself if his brother had not gone before him. Although there were plenty of brothers, even twins, serving in Vietnam at the same time, having a brother in-country meant you were not required to go. (Some of the nurses who volunteered for Vietnam did so precisely in the hopes that their brothers would not have to go.) So when Luther got drafted, he wound up in Germany. And of course he had to consider himself lucky. But as time passed, he came to regret that things had turned out the way they had, and this was his feeling today. It was not just guilt, it was the sense that he had missed out on something. "Every time I see one of those movies I think, shit, why didn't I volunteer? What was the matter with me? I was a soldier, there was a war on, it was where I belonged. I mean, hell, look at my brother. He came back alive, got so much shrapnel in him he sets off the metal detector when he comes to visit, but other than that he's doing great. Got a good job, nice wife and kids." (Luther's own wife had left him upon his arrest, swearing that he would never see his two daughters again even if she had to move them to another country.) "Never in any trouble anymore, though he was a lot tougher kid than I was—he was a hard case. Came back with a bunch of medals—what did I come back with? A beer gut I've never been able to get rid of. Who knows, maybe being in the shit, being tested like that, would have been good for me, too. Might have kept me from fucking up." (But haven't I heard somewhere that a quarter of all U.S. prison inmates are Vietnam vets?) "Hell. Even getting blown away might have been better than—"

"Picture?" It is the young, bucktoothed Jaycee who is always to be found in the visiting room, going from group to group, taking Polaroid snaps for a fee. I am used to him now, but the first time I saw him I was taken aback. All I could think of was traveling with G., how everywhere we went we were pestered by one of these guys aiming a Polaroid, never letting us forget for a second that we were tourists. In France, in Spain, in Italy. And now here . . .

Luther starts to wave the photographer away, but I stop him, saying no, wait, why not? We've never had our picture taken before. I'd like to have a picture.

I hunch over the table where Luther and I are sitting and on whose surface the glistening wet photograph lies. My face emerges with a smile, but Luther's expression is a shock to me: the image of a man utterly forsaken. I glance up then and see that he is not watching the photograph, he is watching me. Same expression. "So," he says. "This is your last visit." No anger. Statement of fact. I drop my glance without a word and stare back at the photograph, whose development is now complete. Cunt and the Man of Sorrows.

When I first got to know Luther again (in high school we went out together for about six months), he said, "Hey, look at my crazy life. You could write about me." Though people say this sort of thing all the time, when they get an inkling that you might actually be thinking seriously of writing something about them they can get pretty nervous. Later Luther said, "If you ever write about me, don't say exactly what it was that put me in here. Even if you change the name, okay? Make up that I did something else."

When we say good-bye, I have to promise him again that his low-down dirty deed is safe with me.

*

After years of struggle—years in which his health grew worse—Chuck finally began receiving disability payments from the VA. He wanted to live somewhere always warm and sunny, he thought he might at least *feel* healthier in such a climate, so he moved to southern California. When Rouenna promised to visit him, he said, Better make it soon. He was sure he was dying.

By this time there had been plenty of other men in Rouenna's life besides Chuck. It seemed that the rule she had lived by during the war—have all the boyfriends you want, love the one you're with, but don't give your heart—had become habitual. Never without a date if she wanted one, usually seeing two or three men at the same time, Rouenna had no desire to settle down with any of them. For about the first ten years, most of the men she dated were veterans. But if these were the men she felt most comfortable with, it was never comfortable enough. Besides, the men she attracted, veterans or not, were never the type to want to settle down, either—at least not with her. Rouenna was not sure why this kept happening. She had always wanted to have a family—right? Or was this yet another thing she no longer remembered correctly? Now here she was twenty-five, here she was thirty. She covered her face with her hands, and when she took them away again thirty was long past and she was still single, and it looked as if she would always be so.

It turned out Chuck's early hunch had been right. Two years after the end of the war, thousands of veterans were applying for disability for health problems they believed were caused by exposure to Agent Orange. Even after they began paying some of these claims, the VA, backed by the Department of Defense, stuck to its story: the herbicides used to defoliate millions of acres of Vietnam were harmless to humans; the health problems suffered by veterans must have some other cause, probably postwar stress. What was indisputable: veterans like Chuck, not yet out of their twenties, were developing the kinds of diseases usually seen only in old people. To the bafflement of his doctors, by the time he left for California, Chuck had the heart, lungs, joints, skin, and eyesight of a man twice his age, and the ravaged liver of a longtime alcoholic, though in fact he had never been much of a drinker. Remembering the group of vets she had seen that time on TV and how much older she had thought they looked than they were, Rouenna was astonished to learn that exposure to dioxin, a toxic chemical contaminant in Agent Orange, could do just that: age you.

After being told at a veterans' hospital that his early symptoms were a type of combat fatigue, Chuck swore never to trust the VA again. The very idea of PTSD made him see red. In the beginning Rouenna thought Chuck was paranoid when he ranted about a government cover-up. But now that she knew that mood swings, depression, and violent rages could all be symptoms of dioxin exposure, she wasn't sure what to think.

"PTSD? Shit," said Chuck. "Know what it really stands for? *Ptsssssssssd.* A spray that can rot every organ in your body, turn you into a homicidal maniac, and give you geek kids."

Rouenna's own health was fine. Her biggest problem was the weight she'd begun to put on after she turned thirty. But it was weight *loss* that was often a symptom of dioxin exposure. She supposed a case could have been made about her appetite. It was not normal to be as she was, hungry all the time, even after a big meal. And if she had another complaint, it was that she sometimes felt more tired than anyone her age had any right to feel. Still, she was as healthy as she had ever been. She had finally stopped smoking. She had lost her taste for pot, she never took any drugs anymore, and though she still drank, sometimes even too much, it was never in the heavy way she had done during and right after the war.

When the VA announced it would offer free Agent Orange examinations to anyone who had served in Vietnam, Chuck told Rouenna she'd only be wasting her time, but she made an appointment anyway. At the VA clinic she filled out a questionnaire and was given a two-minute exam by a young doctor who told her that, since she had no symptoms of dioxin poisoning now, she could rest assured that she would never have any. And, in answer to her most urgent question: "Go home and have as many babies as you want."

About a month later, Rouenna received a letter from the VA saying that there had been no spraying in the areas where she had been stationed in Vietnam—a lie. Defoliants were used around the perimeters of all base camps, and during the twelve months of Rouenna's tour the spraying of Agent Orange, which was not stopped until late 1970, had been at its height. Though she had not been a trooper like Chuck, who spent weeks moving through spray-drenched boonies, breathing tainted mist and drinking tainted water, anyone who'd been anywhere in South Vietnam during the war had at least something to worry about, and among those now asking for disability were veterans who'd never set foot in the field.

In Vietnam she had never cared, never once stopped to ask herself, Hey, if that shit can kill every leaf in the jungle, what must it be doing to me? No one had, that she recalled. When you've got the immediate effects of white phosphorus right under your nose, you don't worry about what the future effects of some weed killer might be. Rouenna could remember laughing like everyone else at the motto of those who flew those spray missions—*Only we can prevent forests*—and thinking it was one of the funniest things she had ever heard.

So far Rouenna appeared to be one of the lucky ones—one of the many who with the passing of time continued to show no sign of damage. But what if she really did do as that doctor said and have as many babies as she wanted—or even just one? Could he promise her no birth defects when there were veterans—including some army nurses—whose babies had been born with many? How safe could Rouenna feel after picking up a news magazine one day and seeing the words *dioxin* and *thalidomide* in the same sentence? Chuck, who said he would never dare father a child, had shown her another article that included a list of birth defects in children born to Vietnamese or American war veterans, a list that had seared itself into her memory like a brand. Babies born with heart defects, or missing parts of their brains or spines. Babies born with missing digits, cleft palate, webbed feet, clubfeet, missing or shortened limbs. Babies born mentally retarded. Babies born with missing organs, double organs, organs growing outside their bodies. Babies born with malformed genitals or with no ears or nose. Babies born with no eyes!

Her mother accused her of overreacting, even of using Agent Orange as an excuse. And because Rouenna knew that most veterans' babies were born with everything just as and where it should be, she sometimes thought her mother was right. She prayed that her mother was right, because she was not yet ready to give up hope of ever marrying and having a child. But there was another question nagging Rouenna. Why did she never fall in love? Fear of Agent Orange could hardly be blamed for that.

In time Rouenna came to believe that she had been fooling herself. She had given her heart after all—not to one man, no, but to all the men she had been with during the war, even those whose names and faces she could not remember. What she did remember was being in love—she had been passionately in love every minute of that year. She had not been in love with anyone like that again since her return, and when she was honest with herself she knew that she would never be.

After Chuck, the most important man in Rouenna's life would turn out to be Aldo, the owner of the steakhouse where she waited on tables. It surprised her at first to find herself in the arms of a man old enough to be her father, though she was not the only young woman attracted to the boss. A thick head of hair and a firm chin had kept Aldo handsome into his sixties. He had a lustrous, well-fed look, he was a gentleman, with old-fashioned courtly ways, he smelled deliciously of bay rum, and he had no trouble at all getting the women he hired to work for him into bed. These trysts usually took place in a hotel—not some flop-house down by the docks or one of those ugly midtown towers full of salesmen but a small inn just off Park Avenue, popular with French and German tourists. Aldo was a romantic—key to his success. He was married, of course. He and his wife, who rarely visited the restaurant, lived in Brooklyn Heights. Pictures of their handsome children and grandchildren hung on the restaurant walls. Though Rouenna appreciated Aldo's suave side and the trouble he took to court a humble waitress, the encounter that excited her most happened in a flash in the kitchen after closing one night when Aldo had had too much bourbon, and involved one of the rose-stained butcher blocks and a stick of butter. Butter. The steakhouse rule was a generous chunk slathered over the hot meat just before it was served. The regulars, the ones at the best tables, got as much as half a stick. Bourbon, red meat, melting butter: for a time it was Rouenna's very definition of pleasure.

And for a time Aldo was enough for Rouenna. Not that he expected her to be faithful to him, and not that they were able to grab much time alone together, but during the three years that they were lovers Rouenna was increasingly less drawn to other men, and if it wasn't love she felt for Aldo it was something close—but this she was not to realize fully until the affair was over.

Though he came in to the restaurant almost every day and swore always to keep working, two heart attacks less than one year apart forced Aldo to retire. The steakhouse was sold and replaced by a sushi place. The house in Brooklyn was sold, and Aldo and his wife moved to Montauk.

For Rouenna, it was a double loss. She missed Aldo more than she would ever have thought. And she had been happy working at the steakhouse; Aldo was good to his employees. Bereft, for the first time in her life Rouenna shied away from men. She would have been celibate had not the Ukrainian electrician who lived across the hall presented himself at her door once a week when his wife went to visit her mother. But the truth was, Rouenna had reached an age when it was no longer so easy to pick up men. One of the last times she had gone to a bar to do just that, she'd been taught a hard lesson. She had plunked herself down confidently next to a cute young guy who was unmistakably looking for company. He ignored her. Rouenna had not had such a humiliating rejection since high school, and when it happened again—same bar, different guy—she took the lesson to heart: This was not Vietnam, and she was not twenty-two and one of only a handful of available round-eyes.

Besides, there were a lot of arguments against picking up strangers these days, the rise of AIDS not the least of them.

The weight that would later get beyond her control came on gradually, and for several years Rouenna could have been seen as her mother had once been seen: fat in all the right places. Aldo certainly saw her that way. And even after she'd put on another ten, fifteen pounds, Rouenna discovered that in a place as big as New York City she wasn't going to have any trouble finding men who did not share the popular taste for thinness, who preferred heft—up to a point. Then Rouenna passed that point. But this happened at a time when she was least concerned about how she looked to men, when she'd had a couple of bad experiences and was down on men as she had never been. Sometimes she blamed Aldo: he had spoiled her. Most of the men she met after him struck her as louts. Or maybe it was just that, once she passed a certain age (or weight), a woman was foolish to expect kindness from men. Then came a night of terror. A man she met at a street fair and brought back to her apartment started to beat her. Who knows what might have happened had not her screams brought to the door her Ukrainian, whose bass-voiced threats and hammering fists sent the bastard fleeing down the fire escape.

After that it was easy to give up sex. (The gallant Ukrainian understood.) Rouenna did not miss it nearly as much as she supposed a healthy woman should. Weeks, months passed, and she spent almost every evening at home alone. Better alone. Better the safety of her room, her clean bed. Better her own slow clean hand. And then even that safe, simple act lost its appeal.

Something was wrong. Should she go to a doctor? Loss of libido: a well-known symptom of dioxin exposure and one of Chuck's many complaints. But though Rouenna could not say what the cause of her problem was, she did not believe it was dioxin.

It was just a phase, she decided. What—did she really think she was never going to have sex again? Ridiculous. A woman not even middle aged. Why, just look at her mother.

If there was a connection between her lost interest in sex and her new interest in cooking, Rouenna did not stop to analyze it; she was not the type. She still had a hole in her stomach. She still could have put away twice as much food as she did. She would have suspected an overactive thyroid except that her pulse was normal and she never lost weight. One thing she could say for sure: She was not alone. Everywhere you looked—newspapers, magazines, TV—you saw something—you saw more and more— about cooking and eating. Rouenna was seduced by the photographs and by the language of food writing (not all of which she understood: in a restaurant review she read about a lamb chop from New Zealand arriving on a chaise of embalsamed spinach). New restaurants and gourmet shops were opening up all over town, including the neighborhoods where Rouenna lived and worked, and she wished she could try them all. She tried as many as she could afford. She liked going out to eat with friends, but she didn't mind eating out alone, either. She did not feel lonely or conspicuous the way she knew many other people did. All you had to do was bring a magazine—you didn't have to read it, just leave it lying open next to your plate. Perhaps partly because it was a sushi restaurant that had replaced her beloved steakhouse, Rouenna never shared in the craze for raw fish, and she thought too much spice killed flavor, but most other food she loved, and for the first time in her life she was willing to be adventurous. Oh, there was a lot more to the world than bourbon, red meat, and butter.

Once she started trying her own hand at recipes, Rouenna found that she preferred cooking to eating out. Eating out was fun, but cooking was a real hobby—the first hobby Rouenna had ever had—and it did for her what hobbies are meant to do: it relaxed her and entertained her and gave her a sense of accomplishment. She was a good cook—probably good enough to earn a living as one, but she was never tempted to do this. No, it was all about pleasure—pleasure and solace. When she was feeling low, nothing could pick her up like preparing some complicated dish from scratch. Nothing could soothe her nerves like a big bowl of homemade soup or spaghetti with clams or spaghetti carbonara. She did not need to be told that cooking was hardly the ideal hobby for someone who was overweight. But she also knew that, were this pleasure and solace to be taken from her, she would not have been able to replace it; she would have been miserable.

She got in the habit of giving dinner parties, more as an excuse to cook than because she enjoyed having company. In fact, she was never comfortable in the role of hostess. She had never been good at small talk, anxiety about whether her guests liked the food spoiled her own appetite, and afterward she was left with a big mess. So she began instead to cook whatever she wanted and give portions away—nothing easier than to give food away, to the church, to her neighbors and to people she worked with, to her mother and her mother's husband whom she visited often. She bought a full set of Tupperware and a large canvas tote bag with sturdy leather handles. "I've got macaroni and cheese today." Nothing easier.

When she finally did go to a doctor (her first time in years), it was for symptoms other than loss of desire, and she was surprised when the doctor himself brought this up. "Surprise" hardly covered what she experienced next, when the doctor began talking about change of life. Rouenna just had to interrupt the man and remind him that she was thirty-nine years old—her *mother* had gone through the change not that long ago. The doctor was one of that cold, distracted, impatient breed that every nurse knows so well. Though it might be a little on the early side, he said, such cases were far from unheard of.

But to Rouenna it was purely absurd, so unexpected, so hard to believe, she could think of only one thing. "I was in Vietnam."

The words sounded hollow and clanking to her ears, like coins or nails dropped onto bare tiles, not just because of her state of shock but because she had not said them in a very long time. Instantly she was bathed in sweat. The doctor stared as if he had not understood. "I was a nurse—an army nurse."

No change in his expression, not a flicker of interest.

"And—well—during the time I was there, I was almost certainly exposed to Agent Orange."

The doctor frowned and shook his head. He didn't have time for this.

"And I was just thinking—wondering—if that could have anything to do with it."

"I don't know anything about Agent Orange," the doctor said. "But I'm sure there's no connection."

"You don't know anything about Agent Orange, but you're sure there's no connection. Hey, you ought to be working for the VA."

"There's no need to get nasty."

"Sorry about that, doc, it's just my PTSD flaring up. Know anything about PTSD? I get these freaky urges sometimes to wring someone's neck."

Once she was sure—and she was sure soon enough—that the doctor was right about what was happening to her, Rouenna no longer cared whether Agent Orange did or didn't have anything to do with it.

"Because, in the end, what difference did it make?"

We were sitting on a blanket spread on the grass. We had just finished eating the picnic that Rouenna had prepared the night before: cold baked chicken, hard-boiled eggs, potato salad, olives and pickles, lemonade, iced tea, and peanut butter cookies. As usual, enough for a whole family—and it was mostly families picnicking around us—lots of kids—which might have been what got Rouenna thinking and talking about this.

"I always thought that was my biggest mistake. I should have had a little faith. I shouldn't have waited. I should have taken the chance. My mother was right, I shouldn't have been so scared. I should have had more faith." It was the sort of thing to bring out her Catholic side, her superstitious side. "At first I thought maybe

I was being punished, because I was so promiscuous for such a long time. And then I started thinking about all those war orphans, those hopeless little kids, I saw them all the time, and it never entered my mind to adopt one—not in a million years would I have brought one of those gook kids back with me. But maybe that was what was supposed to happen, maybe that's what God wanted me to do: save one of those babies' lives. A test, and I failed it—you know what I'm saying? So now I was being punished by never having a kid of my own." I hated it when she talked like this, but I let her go on. "There were a lot of do-gooders in Nam, relief workers, religious types, and they were always trying to get people to help, to take one of those abandoned or sick kids off their hands. I couldn't imagine doing such a thing then. But now, every time I see someone like those two guys who live in the next building"—a gay couple who had adopted a little Chinese girl—"I think, well, look at that. If *they* could do it.

"Anyway, I waited too long. And when that doctor told me what was up and I had to face the fact that I'd missed my chance for good, I thought I would die. For a while I could hardly get myself out of bed in the morning. But I made it, you know. I got through. I survived."

We were both silent then, and I was surprised when after a short time she broke the silence with a laugh. Her funny backward laugh. "You should have seen the look on that fucking doctor when I said that about PTSD."

It was a beautiful day, one of the most glorious days of what had been a glorious fall, and we were in a beautiful place, a place that had come immediately to mind when, a few days before, Rouenna called me and said, "You know what I'd really love to do? Go for a drive in the country. To see the leaves—I want to go somewhere and see the coloring of the leaves. Would you like to do that with me? We could take my car. I could make us a picnic." The Hudson Valley, the leafy grounds of what was once a huge private estate—there stood the grand house still, a museum now (a museum *then*, some would have said), also open to the public, guided tours only. Magnificent views of mountains, river, and sky. Saturday, many visitors, some to tour the house, others to picnic, and no fewer than five bridal parties to pose for photographs. A perfect day so far, except for one terrible moment when a trio of small boys approached, pointing and giggling and chanting away. "Fat*so*. Les*bo*. Fat*so*. Les*bo*." Not the first time something like this had happened to us, and I didn't know what to do, I thought my head would burst, I thought my heart and lungs would burst, it seemed to go on for hours though it was really almost at once that a man in a tartan tuxedo (he was in one of the bridal parties) came and called them off.

"Hey, don't be so sensitive, they're just dumb kids," Rouenna said, tossing me a pack of tissues.

The leaves were no longer at their peak—it was the last week of October—but there was still plenty of foliage and plenty of color to admire, mostly various hues of yellow and brown. Rouenna pointed to a patch and said that was the color the leaves would turn after they had been sprayed and before they fell from the trees. There were people who thought it was called Agent Orange because the leaves changed color, she said, but in fact it was because the barrels the defoliant came in were marked with an orange stripe. When she told me there were others, Agent Purple, Agent Blue, Agents Green and Pink and White, I thought she was joking, of course, but she shook her head. "I shit you not. Had a whole goddamn rainbow of weed killer over there." She explained how it worked, how something in the spray would force the cells in the plants to keep growing and growing until they grew themselves to old age and death.

"Chuck told me about humping through areas, these spooky ghost forests in which every green thing was dead and dead birds fell out of the trees and dead fish bellied up in the ponds. And the men would wash up in that water, and they would fill their canteens and drink it. I've heard some assholes say, Well, how stupid can you be, it was their own damn fault. People don't understand, there are things you don't stop to think about in a war. Besides, those men were thirsty."

I asked her how she thought Chuck was doing now, and she said, "Last time we spoke, he was feeling pretty weak, he wasn't getting around much anymore." But that had been more than ten years ago.

She never made it out to California for that visit.

The trip to the Hudson Valley would take on more and more significance for me as time went by. For one thing, that was the most time Rouenna and I ever spent together in one day, and I saw her only once after that. I would remember that, in spite of talking about mistakes and regrets, Rouenna seemed quite happy and at peace with the world that particular day, or at least as happy and peaceful as I had ever seen her. (*I made it. I got through. I survived.* Her funny backward laugh.) Later, I would go over the day in my head countless times, and all kinds of things jumped out at me. For example, at one point that afternoon she brought up the war, and she said, "Okay, I'll tell you two more stories." It was the "two more" that jumped out later. Two more—meaning two last, two final? Now, of course, it is impossible for me to hear those words any other way. *These are the last two stories about Vietnam that you'll ever hear from me*—for such they turned out to be. But had Rouenna known this?

And another thing she said that day (I believe it was after she told me those last two stories, but I'm not sure): "You know, if you ever want to use any of the stuff I told you, it's okay." It was clear what she meant: if I wanted to use any of her stories for my own purposes, I could. She gave her permission.

And I remember how I had to control myself when she talked about being punished by God—she knew how much I hated that kind of talk. Another time, another day, I had told her about a woman I once met on my way home from a dance class—I was still living on Staten Island at the time; in fact, I met this woman on the ferry. She was from Buenos Aires and she had a sister who'd been a big star there, with the Ballet Argentina. Paralysis struck this thriving prima ballerina. "And we all knew why: it was because being a dancer meant everything to her, even more than having children, she always said she would never have children, and God heard her and He punished her." Imagine, I said to Rouenna. There you are, your life destroyed, you're sitting in a wheelchair, surrounded by your family, and you know that every time they look at you, *that's what they're thinking.* To me it was one of the most fiendish stories I'd ever heard, and I was outraged all over again when Rouenna just shrugged and said, "Yeah, but God really does do things like that."

On the day we drove upstate to see the leaves, this also happened. We were in the car, we were almost there, we were talking, and I slipped and said "Roro."

"'Roro'! Who's that? Where do you get off calling me that?"

"I'm sorry."

"I hate that name. I've always hated it. Spent half my life try-ing to get away from that dumb name. The whole time I was growing up, I was always begging my family not to call me that, but they just went ahead anyway, and it really pissed me off." She was pissed off now; I could tell by the way she was driving. "In school, what do you think? Rhymes with *dodo*, just what a kid needs. And after I got left back, you can imagine how oversensi-tive I was about that. Rhymes with *yoyo*. Not to mention 'Roro, row your boat.' Shit. I got that all the time. Once I was big enough, anytime someone got it into their head they could call me that, I'd straighten them out right off the bat. Bad enough I still can't get my mother to stop. *So don't you now go start calling me Roro!*"

"I said I was sorry."

"How would you like it if I called you—"

"I'm sorry, Rouenna! I promise I'll never do it again!"

"It's a sore spot."

"No. Really?"

"In Nam everyone had a handle—Pretty Polly, Grub, the Beaver, Killer Joe—but not me. I made it clear I wanted people to call me by my real name only."

"It's a beautiful name." A name I had never heard before and that I figured was a variant of Rowena. "This is our exit."

She survived. Childhood. Vietnam. Post-Vietnam. Never marry-ing. Never having children. Change of life. "But I don't care what that doctor said, it was too early." And though she knew she was being irrational, she couldn't help feeling ashamed. She didn't want anyone to know, she didn't tell anyone, not one girl-friend, not her mother. She didn't want to feel like a freak, and she didn't want anyone's pity. In fact, it was during this time that she went further in the direction she was already tending toward after she lost Aldo: she kept more and more to herself. It wasn't that she didn't get along with most people, she was not antisocial ("I got no use for misanthropes"). It was just that time spent by herself was, well, more relaxing than time spent with others— and this was true more and more. And it was not just *sexual* desire that had become a thing of the past. Rouenna had few desires anymore, very few things she could name that she had strong feelings about. Unlike most people, she didn't measure herself against others, envy of other people and the things they might have was a feeling that seldom visited her—she had never been the envious type. And she was not looking for excitement, she'd had her share of excitement, she was not asking for much from life at this age, all she wanted was peace. So: going to work and coming home to have dinner, watch a few hours of TV, and go early to bed—she was not going to complain about boredom, what was the point? Going out with a friend now and then, driv-ing out to Jersey (even more often now that heart disease had made an invalid of her mother's husband), visiting her brother and his wife and four kids in Louisiana every couple of years— was this really so different from or worse than other lives? She doubted it.

(I once stole a peek at the pocket diary being examined by a woman sitting next to me on the bus. She had written one word in the space for each day of the week. For Monday through Fri-day, she wrote "Work." For Saturday and Sunday, "Off.")

It was true that there had been one excruciatingly bad spell Rouenna had had to endure, about a year and a half during which she experienced fits of restlessness and discontent that were beyond any relief. She was reminded of a time when she was still in the army: she was taking a shower when the pump broke and the water went off, leaving her covered with soap. For several hours she had to wait around like that, all tight-skinned and itchy, ready to shriek. That was the feeling she had during this bad spell. Wanting to scratch her own skin right off, ready at every moment to shriek. During this time she drank every night, she put on yet another ten pounds, she even started to smoke again. Something had to be done. To begin with, find a new job. One day on the crowded subway going home from work, she stood squeezed against a man who asked her if she worked in a pet store. When she asked him how he'd guessed, he said, "I smell hamsters." The next day she was looking at the want ads, and two weeks later she started in sales at the clothing store. One move led to another. It didn't matter how lucky she was to have that wonderful Kips Bay apartment, she had been there too long, she felt the walls closing in. But the safer, nicer neighborhoods of Manhattan were now way beyond her means, so she looked to Brooklyn. And with this she took her time, she didn't want to rush into anything, she reminded herself that the next place she moved to could be her home for—well, it was a year before she found the one-bedroom in Williamsburg. A smart move: she was instantly happier. And wasn't it ironic (her mother sure thought so): now that it was a certainty that Rouenna would never have a family, for the first time ever out came an instinct for nest-feathering. It was like a whole new hobby to go with the cooking:

shopping for furniture, linens, rugs—she had decided when she moved to get rid of the same old stuff she'd been staring at for so many years and to buy everything new. Once the least domestic of women, Rouenna now threw herself into creating a cozy, attractive home. She spent her lunch hours wandering Macy's housewares and home furnishing floors and her evenings poring over catalogs from places like Conran's and Pottery Barn—the same catalogs she used to throw away without even opening, junk mail. And once she had everything the way she wanted it, for the first time, too, Rouenna discovered the pleasures of good housekeeping. Everything in its place, everything clean. Not nearly as much fun as cooking, of course, but in its own way soothing; satisfying.

And so the move to Brooklyn brought a brighter period for Rouenna. She had been working as a saleswoman for about a year and a half when she was promoted to store manager. A new apartment full of pretty new things, a new job—and a whole new wardrobe! One night instead of cooking she stopped at a Chinese take-out place near her building. After eating her moo goo gai pan, she cracked opened a fortune cookie and read: *The worst is now behind you.* There was another fortune cookie: every order came with a packet of two. Rouenna was superstitious. She threw the other cookie away.

At the college where I was visiting, interest in the Vietnam era was said to be strong and steadily growing, as it was said to be at colleges all over the country. But I noticed that the books about the war that I checked out of the library had not been checked out in recent years. Most of them had been checked out only once or twice since the library acquired them.

In one of those books, I read that trouble with memory—confusion, lapses, black holes—was another possible symptom of dioxin poisoning.

Two more stories.

The first of the two stories Rouenna told me that day of the picnic was the one about the nurse who got raped in Chu Lai. (*Turn your head you're dead.* No sensitive plants.)

And this was Rouenna's last story:

"We were in the middle of a really big push, we had bodies piling up all over the place. Anyway, they brought this one guy in, and he was bad, shrapnel wound every couple of inches, and he'd lost one of his arms. And he was in such a state about that arm, he kept screaming, *Where is it, where is it, oh help me, my arm, find my arm*—hysterical. He thought he was going to die, and for some reason he was terrified of dying without that arm. Someone said something about it being because of his religion, but I didn't know what religion he was, all I knew was that he was freaking everyone out and something had to be done. So I ran to the place outside the OR where we dumped the parts, we threw them into this big drum until the corpsmen got a chance to burn them. At that time the drum was full—I knew it would be—and I reached in and grabbed an arm that had been cut off at the shoulder like the other guy's—this one was still in its fatigue sleeve, it was a little puffy and perfectly stiff—and I ran back to the guy's gurney. He looks up at me like I was some kind of angel. Is that my arm? he says, just like a little boy. And I tell him a white lie, Rouenna's hundredth little white lie. I say yes, honey, yes, yes, and I gently lay down the arm—it went through my mind how it was like bringing a baby to a new mother—and he hugs that arm tight to himself and he starts to sob. He was sobbing, but at least he was calm now, and a few minutes later he died. He died cuddling that arm.

"Now, what you have to understand is how chaotic the whole scene was. When I went to get the arm, I just grabbed one without thinking, and it turned out to be someone's right arm when the arm that this kid was missing was his left—or maybe it was vice versa, I don't remember. Well, luckily, in the state he was in, the kid never noticed. But later we kept cracking up over that.

"Some people thought it was weird to do what I did, but you can't tell me it was wrong. Whatever you could do to help those poor kids, that's what you had to do."

Whose woods these are whose woods these are whose woods these are—

She said: "I got no reason to be jealous of anyone in this world. I figure I had something in life most people will never have. In one year I think I lived more than most people do even if they live to be a hundred. And all you got to do is look at how things turned out, look at how people think about the past today. Everyone knows that for our generation Vietnam was the big event. Not seeing the Beatles at Shea Stadium or being at Woodstock or the Summer of Love. Not marching around with some sign, sticking your tongue out at the cops, shutting down some stupid college, or blowing up some stupid ROTC building. It wasn't about dropping out or being outrageous, joining an ashram or a rock band. It wasn't about how long you could grow your hair or how much acid you could eat and still keep your brain. All of that seems so diddly-squat now, doesn't it." Yeah. "But not Vietnam.

Vietnam changed this country forever. It was the biggest thing that happened to us, and some of us were actually there. And then you have to think about my own special case—I mean, how many women got to go to Nam?" How many indeed? No one seems to know. No reliable documentation for the exact number of women who served in Vietnam exists, and the range of estimates is remarkable. "And free love? Hey, I got to sleep with more men—more gorgeous young men—than most other women do in their dreams. And let me tell you, sex was as intense as everything else that happened in Vietnam, it didn't matter how inexperienced most of those kids were.

"And think about this: I was the last person some of those men ever saw, the last face they laid eyes on, the last voice they heard, the one they spoke their last words to. Like we used to say: pretty heavy. I can tell you all this because I know you won't think I'm just bragging or waterbullshitting. I wouldn't say these things to a lot of people because they might misunderstand. But the truth is, I am proud of what I did over there. I helped save people's lives, and I helped the ones who couldn't be saved to die—talk about heavy. I was there for those boys when no one else was. And believe me, I gave all I had. The guys' hearts weren't in the war, everyone knows that, that was part of the tragedy and why we lost. But the nurses? Me? I gave them all the heart I had.

"Oh, I tell you, it was something. People have no idea. Yeah, it was hell, it was crazy, it was worse than my worst fears told me it was going to be, and I was blessed to be a part of it. That's how I've always seen it and how I still see it, that won't change. And I don't have to be talking about it all the time. I don't have to tell the whole world about it. I don't need a memorial or a parade or a twenty-one-gun salute. I just want to hold on to some of those memories. I don't ever want to forget how much love I felt and how happy I was then. People don't understand that, but people just have no idea. If they did, they'd be the ones who'd be jealous—of me. *I was there.*"

Once, after she had been talking about the war at some length, she startled me by saying: "Oh, I just wish that you could have been there, too." And then, more vehemently, in a way that moved me almost to tears: "If only we could have been there together!"

I had hoped that writing about Rouenna would bring solace, and of course many times it has. But how often since I began have I looked up from my work and thought, My god, I am so unhappy.

Fat*so.* Les*bo.*

Cunt!

Her funny backward laugh.

Work. Work. Work. Work. Work. Off. Off.

The lingo has always made me cringe. Grunt, hump, boonie, expectant, train wreck, crispy critter, gork. Rear echelon motherfucker, or REMF. Fucking new guy, or FNG. Charlie, the Cong, the Nam. Gook, dink, slope, slant, et cetera. Boo koo. Boom boom. Number one, number ten. Thousand-yard stare, million-dollar wound. Mamasan, papasan. World of hurt. In the shit. Greased, zapped, et cetera. The more I hear these words, the more I hate them.

"Virginia Woolf? She's the one Elizabeth Taylor played in that movie, right?"

———

My mother said, "No, no, no, you've got it all wrong. You didn't see what happened, you weren't even there. And it didn't happen in the Big Playground. It happened in the little playground outside our building."

Two more stories.

Soon after I moved back to New York, I looked up someone I used to know long ago, on Staten Island, and now it was my turn to say, "I don't know if you remember me."

"Don't be silly. I remember every girl I proposed to. Call it a gift. What kind of trouble are you in?"

"What makes you think I'm in trouble?"

"When you're a cop and you don't hear from someone for thirty years and they call you out of the blue, chances are they're calling with some kind of problem."

"It's not really a problem. I'm just trying to find someone." And I explained.

"You try the Internet?"

I had. No luck. "I figured you'd know what to do."

"Yeah. But I'm not exactly supposed to be doing it. So what's this for?"

I explained that it was for something I was writing.

"Oh, yeah. I heard something about that, that you became a writer. But—like what do you write? Stories? Like what kind of stories—love stories?"

"Yes." The only kind worth telling.

"Give me a week," he said. But it was only a day before he called back.

"Helga Paulina di Venere of Minneapolis, Minnesota, died

of breast cancer in 'eighty-nine. Worked on and off as a public school nurse. Never married but she had one kid, male. At the time she died, she was living with her brother."

"Thanks, Lorenzo."

"That's it?"

"That's it. I just wanted to know what happened to her."

"Doesn't sound like you got much of a story there. Now, *my* life, on the other hand . . ."

June. A wedding in East Hampton, my first big social event in more than a year. I meet many people whom I know but have not seen in so long they greet me with "Hello, stranger" and "Where have *you* been hiding?" A lavish affair—three hundred guests—and I am thrilled to be one of them. Such an atmosphere of elegance and gaiety, it makes my head spin. A mansion of incredible grace, designed by the famous architect who happens also to be the one responsible for introducing bride and groom, both former students of his. There are masses of flowers and flowerlike women and men as ravishing as women, all beautifully dressed. We are far away from the world in which I have been immersed. Not a tartan tux, not a fat person, not a Vietnam vet to be seen. There is grilled lobster. There are peaches in champagne. There is a pool, there is the sea. There is a radiant blue sky perfectly matching the blue silk of the bridesmaids' dresses. And there is G. Welcome back to the land of the living, he says, and I want to tell him how right he is. For I have spent too long with the dead, too long alone and unhappy, and now I am thrilled to be a part of this celebration, to be here among the living, the beautiful living.

It is all right seeing G. I had known that he would be here, too, and it is all right between us now, after so much time. We talk and we dance and we drink a lot of champagne. After the cake has been cut and served, we slip away, we go down to the beach and we take off our shoes and walk in the cool sand near the water. We are easy and relaxed together, so much so that as we walk we quite naturally take each other's hand. (Later I will think that perhaps we owed at least some of this ease together to all that champagne.) As we walk I am reminded of something. There is something I want to ask G., a question I could never quite bring myself to ask him before. But now that it is over between us, I feel different. Still I hesitate, knowing how strange it will sound. But hey, this is G. He knows me. So I go ahead and ask. Has he ever tortured or killed some helpless animal just for fun?

His horror is genuine. How could I ask him that? Of course he has never done anything of the kind! What on earth made me even think to ask him such a question?

Oh dear. That note of exasperation oh so familiar to me. Poor G. Driving him crazy had been so easy.

I loved him for his noble face, and for his honesty.

A few minutes later, when we have turned to walk back to the house, he says: "Now, you said animal, right? Like, not including insects."

A group of us takes the train back to the city together, and when we arrive at Penn Station someone suggests we continue the party by going to a club. I want to go along, I really do. I have not had such a good time in ages. But I have to get up early the next day, so I say good-bye and go home alone.

When I get home, though, instead of going straight to bed, I look through some papers on my desk for a letter that came in the mail a few days ago. From Luther.

———

Please don't think I don't understand about your not wanting to come visit anymore because I do, but I was hoping at least I could still write to you and that sometimes you would write me back. You don't have to answer every letter, but it would mean a lot to me if we could stay in touch. Anyway, I will respect your decision whatever it is, it's a free country and all, but if in fact we are not going to be in touch anymore there are some things I want to say. Number one: Don't go being like so many other people and think that you know who I am, because you don't know anything. I have never sat down and told you my whole story from beginning to end and therefore of necessity much of who I am and what I am all about is just a big question mark to you. You take my life since I got here, which I have never told you or anyone else about. People think they know what "life behind bars" is like from watching movies and TV, but in fact they don't know shit. I was thinking about what you told me last time you were here, about that friend of yours and everything you said she had been through. I could tell from the way you talked about her that this person really got to you. And don't get me wrong, I respect your feelings and all, but a nurse in Vietnam, excuse me, that just doesn't seem like such a big deal to me. I mean it's not like she was in combat. And you want to talk about being in the shit, you want to talk about a world of hurt, man, what do you think I am going through every day inside here? I could tell you stories, too. Stories to break your heart. Stories to curl your hair. And talk about needing someone to talk to—talk about needing a friend. Not to put too fine a point on it, this Rowinski friend of yours is dead. Me, I'm not dead, even if everyone's decided to see it that way. I'm not dead, but I am buried. I'm buried alive. It's like a movie I once saw, scariest fucking thing, some guy buried alive in a coffin and he's lying in there screaming and banging and kicking his feet, but no one can hear. People are walking right over the ground where this poor fuck is buried and no one can hear him. Well, let me tell you, that is just what it feels like being in here.

And there is something else that's been on my mind that I need to say though I'm not sure how you are going to take it. But the fact is, if it wasn't for me, you would be dead yourself. Or do you not recall a certain party many many years ago when a certain young lady, namely you, was about to get into a car with a certain Jimmy Adonis who crashed not two minutes and two miles later into a steel fence? Had you been in that car you would most surely have gone through the windshield. But you were not in that car, and why? Because I saw the both of you leaving together and I said to myself, This may not be any of my business, but no way am I going to let that girl get in that car with that totally fucking drunk asshole Adonis. And I stopped you. And Jimmy and I had words about it, but I didn't care. I stopped you, and I made sure you got home safe that night, because I took you there myself. Not that it was all that comfortable for me, walking back to the car through the projects alone at that hour of the night, but I figured I had a duty. You were not my girlfriend (yet) but you were a girl and you were my friend and friends are supposed to look out for each other. And I've been thinking about this a lot since last time I saw you and wondering if you think about those days anymore too. So long ago. Fucking Staten Island. Fucking high school. Football. Victory parties. Those guys—Jimmy and Sherry and Curtis and Angela and Pete. You and me. Tell you the truth, I had forgotten all about that particular night until after your last visit. Then I thought about how you said "You owe me." And then I remembered, and that's when I thought, hey, wait a minute, come to think of it, you *owe* me. *I saved your life.*

There is more. There is much more. Luther always writes thick letters. But I stop reading, I fold the letter in half and I put it with my keys on a shelf near the door. Tomorrow I will take it with me to read on the long bus ride to the prison.